T0146678

IT'S HAULING US

JOSHUA C. NUNNO

authorHOUSE®

AuthorHouse™
1663 Liberty Drive
Bloomington, IN 47403
www.authorhouse.com
Phone: 1 (800) 839-8640

Published by AuthorHouse 07/16/2018

ISBN: 978-1-5462-4230-7 (sc)
ISBN: 978-1-5462-4229-1 (e)

Print information available on the last page.

This book is printed on acid-free paper.

CONTENTS

INTRODUCTION

In the 1850s, the United States whaling business was at its peak, and the dangerous trade of hunting the larges mammal in the world was being slaughtered by the bravest hunters ever brought to sea, but as time went by with new industrial growth, with the need for quick and cheap oil being processed from the ground, the sales of whale oil began to decrease. The ship owners and captains were determined to keep the whale hunting business up and going.

One of many of America's most significant whale fisheries was the Nantucket whaling fleet. The fastest well-built vessel in the fleet was the WS Mako, captained by Calais Gerard and a 30-man crew.

In late 1859, the Mako made a southward course after resupplying in Hawaii. It sailed for the whaling grounds off the Marshall Islands. Her hold had little filling after nine long months passing the Atlantic and Eastern Pacific; the whalers had to take the hunting to more remote areas of the sea making the journey long, harder and dangerous.

This sea tale, however, will not just be of whale hunting, but an account of leadership, courage, survival, and passion.

A story of several crew members that embarked on a long and dangerous voyage across the South Pacific, with the assistance of a young whale calf.

CHAPTER 1

LEADING THE HUNT

On top of the mast pit, stood a young sailor by the name of Charlemagne "Charlie" Evekins. With his sharp eyes, he spotted little spouts from a far distance from the shade of the clouds. Light blue water spouting out from whale's blowholes, he kept his eyes locked onto the source, upon seeing blackfin tails waving out like giant slapping hand fans, it was clear to him, and he made the cry.

"THAR SHE BLOWS! Off to Starboard! Thar She Blows!"

The crew came running out from the galley up to the main deck to see their prey.

Looking through the spyglasses, the Captain and first mate spotted over a dozen black-gray flukes and squirting spouts of mist shooting out of the surface.

"Bring us about!" yelled Captain Gerard, the second mate Mr. Tisburn piloted the vessel and quickly turned the Mako closer to the pack of whales.

When less than a mile away Captain Gerard yelled.

"Lower boats and get after them, lads!"

The men ran all around the deck, preparing the four whaleboats and gathered all the equipment.

First mate Isaac Branter was lowered first, along with the Captain's right behind him, to the other side of the ship was the second mate Tisburn, and the third mate Mr. Fralhem.

As most of the crew were climbing down to the boats.

Evekins climbed off the mast to the deck and ran from one side to another, begging to be let board a boat.

Captain Gerard and Branter were already gone, and Tisburn refused to let him aboard. The kid finally walked to the last boat, with Fralhem yelling out orders in a strong Norwegian accent.

"Get us down you slugs! Get me down and out there!"

With no request or hesitation, the boy just claimed down into Fralhem's boat.

The fourth boat was down in the water, and the hooks were untied. The boats were free.

"Let's get ourselves a whale, venns!" Yelled Fralhem.

The third mate discovered he had another hand on his boat, but instead of making Charles return aboard the ship, he ordered him to grab the spare oar, so they had an extra rower, causing his boat to move faster.

The four boats were rowing off from the Mako, with Branter's passing the captain. Mr. Tisburn held a grip on the steering oar as he points out to the waving flukes of the sperm whales ahead.

"Pull my boys; a jackpot of liquid gold is out there!" yelled Tisburn. "They're waving us to come and get 'em! Pull boys!"

"Oh, we're gaining on them!" shouted Fralhem. As they started passing Tisburn's boat.

"Sneaky Scandy," said Tisburn, chuckling with his pipe.

Fralhem soon gained upon Gerard's boat as the mate, and his crew turned their heads to look towards the captain. Evekins could see anger, jealousy, and even hate in his captain's eyes now that the lowest officer of was beating him.

"Come on you scum, koof idiots!" yelled Gerard. "Bring me up to the whales, don't let them land lovers beat us! Get after them! Get after them!" Mr. Branter's boat came up to a breaching whale, his harpooner took up his weapon, then struck at it. At that split second of being hit like a dart striking in a person's back, it made the giant creature screech like a slaughtered cow and hauled the whaleboat faster than a racing stallion.

Fralhem finally passed by Gerard's boat, as Evekins looked behind to get a glimpse of the pod.

"No, do not look, Charlie, just keep your eyes on me, and stay to the rowing," said Fralhem. The other six rowers were like his own Viking longship crew. His deep rumbling strong tone voice was like a battle drum.

Squirts of seawater shot from the surface like volcanic steam.

Fralhem's boat was gaining up to a full-grown bull.

To the bow seat sat the harpooner Mat Canonchet, looking to Fralhem the third mate who cracked a broad smile and nodded his head. Mat nodded back.

The Pequot native stood from his seat at the very end of the long boat readying his weapon.

"In with the oars lads," said Fralhem." Don't look ahead yet."

All the five others kept with the oars and their eyes glued to the mate.

Below came the giant sperm whale, breaching to the surface on the port side nearly flopping the whaleboat, and almost frightening all men aboard. Canonchet kept his weapon in hand, and with a strong toss, he struck the harpoon into the whale's starboard side.

The startled beast then pulled the boat, and Fralhem shouted with laughter. "Now look to him, boys! We've got him now boys! He's ours!"

All rowers turned around to see the long tight line now being pulled off fast by the panicked whale.

Its tail splashed up water, making it rain down on the boat crew.

Evekins smiled ear to ear as he was on his very first Nantucket sleigh ride, riding faster over the waves than a steam train.

For the past nine months, he had served aboard the Mako as a ship-keeper just tending the ship, firing up the try works, bringing up the butcher tools and coopering oil barrels. The whole time he had longed to be on a boat to witness a whale hunt; after nearly a year, late in that autumn of 1859, his wish came a true.

Within less than an hour, that only felt likes seconds to the crew aboard Fralhem's boat, the bull's strength ran out as it lost of so much blood. The mate made his way to the bow with his lance.

"Clear the way lads, it's getting weak," said Fralhem. Switching positions with his harpooner Canonchet took the steering oar.

Fralhem makes it up to the front bowl end of the boat with a long, razor-sharp lance.

"Put the oars back out, oars back out," ordered Canonchet, since the whale stopped pulling.

The crew paddled closer to the dying beast. Passing long yard after yard, Fralhem ordered two of his rowers to haul in the line as they were getting closer.

The whale made light flaps with its tail, and loud noises were made of soft moans and groans like a bear.

Blood started oozing out from his side coming down its eyebrow, and all the rest of its massive body. Like a red stream turning the blue sea dark red.

Evekins stares deep into the stony eye of the dead giant. Feeling complete sorrow for the poor creature and feeling it had suffered worse than the men.

The rest of the crew laughed and cheered as Fralhem drove his lance down deeper into the whale's body, stabbing it through the lungs, making his blowhole spout out gallons of blood.

"The chimneys of fire!" shouted the whole boat crew. The whale was dead with praises of red blood coming down on their faces and clothes.

CHAPTER 2

TRIPLE BUTCHERY

Hours past and the day turned to dark as Fralhem's boat returned to the vessel with a 60-ton dead whale.

Lights gleamed off the ship's lamps, like a giant floating lantern. Thick fogs of smoke blowing up off the ship's try work house, with three dead whales strapped on both sides of the ship.

Branter's kill was the first being butchered; another was Gerard and Tisburn's who had slain a female and had it strapped to the other side.

In all, the crew killed three whales in one day.

The entire night, all the Mako crew worked without rest. Butchering all the whale carcasses. It was tiring, smelling and messy with large organs and dead fish and squid from the dissected stomachs over the deck as though a monster had regurgitated its meal.

Despite the crew's footwear, some fell on the bloody deck. Some slipped into the piles of the sticky, slimy guts and organs, and had to crawl to the railing to climb back up.

Off the ship, the harpooners armed with spears stood on the dead floating whale carcasses trying to keep sharks from eating all the blubber flesh. The sharks were relentless and swarmed by the dozens chomping off large chunks of whale leaving plate sized bite marks. Back aboard the messy ship, old Prestern the steward with Connell the carpenter helped with boiling the blubber into oil and pouring it into the barrels. Half the crew was flensing off large strips of whale blubber, almost the size of bed mattresses. The other half of the crew, with the help of the mates, cut off the whale's giant head.

Fralhem, with a razor sword, cut open the head from the blowhole to the frontal skull. He then ordered Charlie and young Heszits to go inside and scoop out bucket loads of the valuable spermaceti while the mates collected whale long banana-sized teeth from the long jaw.

Seagulls clouded in the skies and up in the rigging picking up scraps of flesh meat. Sharks swarmed in the water all around the ship feasting on the remains of the whale's body. The blood polluted the water all around the Mako, large pieces of fat had bite marks and teeth stuck in the flesh that some crewmen collected.

The next morning came, and the Mako crew had finally finished what was left of the third whale of Falhem's kill.

In total, the blubber cut from the whales had harvested a total of 119 oil barrels.

At midday, the crew celebrated with an entire day of nothing but a good long sleep down in the forecastle. After they changed out from their red blood-stained clothes into their soft white clean long johns, all the crew crashed into their bunks.

Two days later, up above on the quarterdeck, Mr. Branter came out to see Mr. Tisburn sharing tobacco with Mr. Fralhem and began smoking their pipes as they manned the helm, steering the vessel.

"Well, shipmates, I congratulate you both on your successful killings," Branter said, coming up from the aft deck steps.

"Congrats yourself Branter, you delivered the first strike, as you did on the first whale, back at the Cape Horn," said Fralhem with Tisburn applauding.

"This should be a record for us, the crew of the Mako

killing a total of three whales in a single afternoon," said Tisburn. "And maybe in the whole history of whaling."

"We've done well my friends," said Fralhem. "So, what did the captain think of our killing spree? Do you think a little grog reward will be in order?" Asked with the second mate cracking grin to the faces, but Branter nodded.

"No, I'm afraid not boys," the first mate replied. "Captain Gerard traded all the alcohol, and rest of the chewing tobacco to the Hawaiians. He wanted me to keep it secret, so it wouldn't upset the crew because he thinks it will help keep strict discipline aboard with sober men."

"Well that's unpleasant, how do you think this crew can celebrate after a good whaling victory and all the challenging work they've done?" asked Tisburn. "Have them just keep eating tasteless biscuits, rotten fruit and salted chowder the whole voyage?"

"I guess Gerard wants no celebration, the captain seems to gain a temper on this voyage," said Branter. "Ever since I killed the first whale and drew first blood he's been all mad-eyed and frowned mouth ever since."

"Guess the captain's jealous, for he had no chance in getting the first strike," said Tisburn.

"Or even more, because his boat was swamped, and he blamed me for not helping him back on," said Fralhem.

"Perhaps he's a petty, unforgiving hothead," said Tisburn.

"Or just an incompetent pissant!" replied Fralhem.

"Now! Now! Watch your mouths men; if you said that in front of the whole crew, the captain would suspect us of mutiny," said Branter. "Besides, as much as our superior is unpopular to us, we must make the best of it and kiss his ass."

"Popular? We should be honest with ourselves; he's a

sour headed, downright blowhard, with his wealthy Pappy that spoiled him rotten and gave him the captain's rank. He cares not for us at all, but himself," said Fralhem, with Tisburn nodding in agreement.

"Watch it, mates, I want to hear no more of this!" said Branter. "Now you both should get some shut eye and get those sea brains to rest, we're going to keep the course southeast, and I need my two veteran sailors well rested."

The two mates went below underneath the steering deck right outside the captain's room.

Gerard had his stern windows open, and Gerard laid awake hearing the grumbling of his officers, speaking all negative about his captaincy.

His head ran with hate, and sadistic torture, wishing he could keelhaul his three mates, but he was powerless knowing how his crew loved and respected the mates.

All he could think was the task of getting the hull filled up and having the ship owners and his father sack and band the three mates out of the whaling company.

Early in the morning, the men awoke for breakfast.

To the rear end of the galley table sat third mate Fralhem.

Evekins sat a mere distance aside watching the mate dine alone picking at his meal and mouthing words to himself.

Evekins decided to pay the officer a visit.

"Good morning Mr. Fralhem," said Charles. Fralhem didn't answer just gave a tiny smile with a nod.

"I never had a chance to thank you for in letting me aboard your boat, sir, and let me take part in the hunt," Evekins said, staring at the mate, who just gave him a bland sea stare with his misty brown eyes. Seconds past and Evekins was about to get up and leave as he thought the made was ignoring him.

"I should be thanking you, Charlie," said Fralhem, "Your

sparseness made my boat faster and got us the second kill, you're quite a strong oarsman."

"Thank you, sir," said Charlie.

"I said I should be thanking you for your volunteering, and for the extra help," Fralhem said passing Evekins his porridge and getting up out of his seat.

"Oh yes, you're welcome sir. It's been my dream to be on a Nantucket sleigh ride."

"Good, I had a dream like that before I started out whaling," the third mate said.

"Where did you start?" asked Charlie. "Aboard the Eriksson of Tonsberg; I was much younger then you when I struck my first whale," Fralhem said before he walked up on deck.

CHAPTER 3

Approaching a Squall

The oldest crew member Thomas Prestern and Kevin Connell were tarring up the cracks in the whaleboats.

Harpooner Canonchet was up in the mast pit, and third mate Fralhem was in his tyrant mode yelling and cursing at the crew to keep scrubbing the deck.

"Keep yourselves down. I want every red blood stain on the deck wiped off!" Fralhem yelled in the ears of two sailors and giving another member a light kick to the rear. As an officer, Fralhem was both admired and feared as sometimes he was like a bully to the crew. Yet he treated every man equal. The mates were brutes but fair, yelling, cursing and physical hits, yet they kept morale high with confident words, jokes, and music.

Mr. Tisburn ordered the cabin boy Jethro Heszits, an orphan from Montauk, along with two other sailors with a flute, fiddle, and lute, to play some sea shanties to lift the crew's spirits.

The music helped the crew through hours of challenging work, with sore knees and bleeding hands from the ropes.

In the mast pit, harpooner Canonchet spotted flukes far off ahead of the bow. Before he was going to split his lungs to cry out, he looks farther forward and saw giant pitch-black clouds. There was no question there was a storm coming.

The Algonquian native took the line and slid down the mast.

"Branter? Branter? He said coming up on the quarter-deck step.

"You've seen something?" Branter asked. "Ay, I saw a pod of whales far ahead to the starboard bow." Before the harpooner finished, Mr. Branter ran up to the bow deck with a spyglass.

Why have you not shouted, 'Thar she blows'?" asked Tisburn running down to inform the captain.

"What else did you see?" asked Fralhem.

Captain Gerard walked out from the deck, "On your feet lads, we're approaching a whale pod."

The crew stood up, on their feet and crowded the bow, seeing the large pod flicking up their tails.

"Ready the boats," Gerard ordered Branter who nodded in agreement, when the Mako was being turned aside.

"What the devil is this?!" asked the captain seeing Fralhem turning the helm.

The captain rushed to the stern, "Fralhem what the hell are you doing?!" said Gerard taking the helm from the third mate. With the other two behind.

"Canonchet spotted a storm cloud ahead and thought it would be too dangerous to take the boats out."

"The storm seems far off, I'm sure we'll have time to make it to the ship," said Branter.

"I wouldn't take that risk sir, I agree with Mr. Canonchet," said Tisburn.

"Oh, flaming rubbish," said Gerard. "We're whalers! the strongest mariners of the sea, we should not let a storm stop us from the hunt, they're all whales out ahead, and I say go aloof."

"Yes sir," said Branter eagerly agreeing. "Away with the boats."

Fralhem looked to Tisburn and Canonchet, each had the unpleasant images of waves they will go against in a massive sea storm.

CHAPTER 4

Whaling in Water Hills

The four boats were lowered and off. The eager mate Branter retook the lead, the captain was close behind, while the other followed in a slow cushion.

The second and third mate, along with their harpooners, did not have their eyes on the whale pod but to the dark clouds approaching the horizon. Like darkness was going to come down on the crew, like a clean sweep that would make everything vanish.

Branter's boat came upon a surfaced whale, out in the open and ready to be harpooned. Before his harpooner was able to make the hit, Captain Gerard cut right into the first mate's boat, hitting the whale first.

"The captain swiped our whale," said a sailor in Branter's boat.

"Never mind that lads, there's plenty out and about," said the first mate, still ignoring the nasty clouds growing over.

Behind, Fralhem ordered his boat to a complete halt and yelled for Tisburn to stop.

"Alright, lads we must return to the ship!" the third mate yelled.

"Aye, better we man the ship then lose her in a storm," Tisburn said to his crew.

The two boats made for the ship.

On the Mako, Evekins watched half the hunting party coming for the ship. He made for the helm looking at his shadow on the deck. Then it instantly disappeared from the darkness, of the black cumulus that had blocked off the sun. The wind kicked up, and rain started to shower down the rigging, sails, and mast onto the deck.

"We have to signal the captain to return ship!" said Prestern getting the pumps ready and ordered Mr. Connell the carpenter to tie everything down below deck. A loud call coming off the ship was Fralhem, he called to Prestern and four other ship-keepers to the railing.

"You men set the mainsail we're going to fish out the captain!" Tisburn ordered.

Far out in the deadly dark waves, Branter's men had struck a whale, pulling off in the dark rain blinding Fralhem's view of the spyglass, back on the Mako. "I can't see Branter!" he said to Tisburn with Evekins assisting the steering wheel.

Up closer to the ship captain Gerard finally, come to his senses that the water was becoming too rough.

He made his harpooner cut the line. The water pushed the long boat up and down and side to side, knocking the Captain on his back, causing him to lose the steering. The captain's boat was now adrift, his men yelled and panicked losing three of their oars.

Gerard didn't try to stand up but stayed huddled down like a coward hiding under his desk, shaking in the flooding water washing all over the bottom of the boat. To Gerard and his crew, all seemed lost until the harpooner shouted, "The Mako! The Mako is coming for us!"

The crew cheered in relief, and the captain climbed up on the boat's railing, shaking like a scared cat.

When Fralhem and Prestern pulled the captain and his boat crew aboard. The men rushed everywhere, now shorting the sail, because of the high winds kicking up making the noise of massive cries and screeches like the howls of a ghost and it has begun to push the Mako down to her port side, on the verge of capsizing her.

Fralhem, Canonchet, and the crew had all the sails cut loose, and they waved in the wind like sizeable white bed sheets from the rigging.

Ropes fluttered all around, whipping the faces of some sailors like loose whips.

Hours through the night the ship was damaged but survived the deadly storm. The two mates and crew worked until dawn, cleaning all areas of the vessel while Captain Gerard went to his cabin. It was such a mess, like a children's playroom, but he cleaned it himself, afraid to ask his angry crew to do it, even look any of them in the eyes.

CHAPTER 5

A Sweep for The Missing Mate

The Mako was in near ruins, with the supplies in the hold scattered all over like it had been raided. Lines and sails hung off the mast like wrinkled tatters of laundry and worse still Mr. Branter's boat was missing.

Gerard finally came out from the cabin. Walking along, the crewmen noticed he had two pistols strapped to his belt that was barely covered by his dress coat as he walked to the bow deck.

"Tisburn?! Fralhem?!" he shouted. The two mates turn as they help to repair the jib sails.

"Where's Branter?" asked the captain.

"When did you last see him?" Fralhem asked.

"That's not what I asked," said Gerard. "Branter disappeared from my sight in the storm, have you spotted him yet?!"

"Do you want us to put out the whaleboats to do a sweep search?" asked Tisburn.

"No, my boats took damage, I want all men on watch from the masts and not to rest until dark," Gerard ordered.

"Aye sir," said both mates.

"Of course, they're damaged," whispered Fralhem before Tisburn could hush him, "and it wouldn't have happened if you listened."

"Fralhem!" yelled Captain Gerard "Report to my cabin!"

The Norwegian officer stood up and avoided eye contact as he followed the commander to the cabin.

As the mate past the working crew, they turned to look at Gerard.

"What are you all looking at?" yelled Gerard. "Clear the deck and to the mast pits, find Branters!"

Fralhem stood in the neat cabin and noticed all the firearms in every corner of the Captain's room as if it looked more like an armory.

In Fralhem's mind, he realized Captain Gerard feared a mutiny and his ill-tempered blowhard captain has turned paranoid.

Gerard came in from behind, closed the door, then walked behind his desk.

"Well now Mr. Fralhem," said Gerard sitting down placing his two pistols on the table. "I don't know how you Scandies run whaling ships or a crew, but I don't think they're anything like the famous Vikings back in their golden ages. If you think it is right to whisper negative phrases and comments about my way of running this vessel, well then, you're more stupid than a fish swimming near a shark," said Gerard.

"Yes stupid, in fact, if the crew trusted me more I'd have them set up a gauntlet to run you through, and even more so if I was an owner like my father, I outrank you. I know how you and the rest of the mates feel about me."

"Ja, as a matter of fac…." Before Fralhem could defend,

Gerard talked over the top of him.

"Shut up Scandy! Just keep your rough, annoying kraut mouth shut and follow my orders. Now get the hell out of here."

Before Fralhem exited the cabin, he turned and said,

"I'm a Norwegian, not a German!" before slamming the

door behind him. Then it bounced open again, making the captain had to stand and close it himself.

All three masts held half the crew while they were looking out on all sides of the horizon for Mr. Branter's boat.

Fralhem sat next to Evekins on the lookout. The mate just looked down with an unhappy exasperation.

Charlie looked around; the sea was light on waves, and the clouds had blown away leaving a beautiful blue sunny sky.

He looked to the deck with crewmen looking from the railings, and Captain Gerard searching with his spyglass, as Tisburn piloted the Mako.

Charlie looks at Fralhem again, but the mate was now covering his face with his hand.

"You know sir? If this was an independent ship, I'm sure a lot of us would vote you as captain, anyone but that squid git Gerard."

Fralhem looked to the man with bright eyes.

"I think you'd make a much better Captain," said Charles.

"As of most this ship thinks."

Well, that's really fine to know, but I would vote for Branter in all fairness, and I think these American country's men would want me," Fralhem said looking out to the sea.

"Don't think like that, America may not all be great, but things change, so don't hate it, you might have a chance; just keep being the way you are."

"I don't hate America; it's a great country, I only hate three things: stupidity, loneliness and above all, abuse of power."

"Like Gerard, right sir?" Charlie asked.

"Yes, that and the hardships that made me leave Norway." Answered Fralhem.

"Why did you leave, other than for the New England whaling?" asked Charlie.

"It was not whaling; I love the life as a whaler, I love sailing, fishing, navy and anything else that keeps me at sea.

Believe it or not but I wasn't even born a seagoing boy, but a landsman," said Fralhem. "Born on a mountaintop in Fjord to a Sami father, and a Danish mother. I hated the land, but ever since I began reading tales of Vikings and their voyages on their great longships, I fell in love."

"But what hardships?" Charlie asked.

"It's too personal and complicated," answered Fralhem.

Charlie just said "Oh" and shook his head, thinking after being confronted by the captain, he was not to talk heart to heart.

"Well I hope we do find Branter," said Charlie.

"Me to Charles," respond Fralhem." You're a good sailor; maybe next time on my boat, I'll have Canonchet teach you to harpoon a whale.

Charlie looked to the mate with an excited face.

"Really?" He asked. Before being interrupted by the mast pit.

"I see Branter!" yelled out Mr. Witty standing with Canonchet.

"Far off to the starboard, I see the boat!" the young African American man yelled and pointed.

Charlie and Fralhem's could see of what looked like a capsized the boat, with waving arms that look smaller than the seagull's swings.

"Come on men, let's get them!" ordered Fralhem, sliding down a rope.

Tisburn and Fralhem lowered boats, to go pick up Branter's men. When they approached the capsized boat, the lost boat crew were wet tired and looked green faced after drifting for two days with no food or water. Now they were finally rescued.

"Thank you, Lord, rescued before we got thirsty!"

Shouted Tisburn.

"Oh God bless you, boys!" Yelled Branter. "We almost got dragged down by a whale. That's the last time I go hunting in a squall." Branter said when pulled into Fralhem's boat.

As the first mate's crew rested in the rescue boats.

Tisburn towed the damaged boat back to the ship.

Gerard watched the crew with his spyglass.

"Captain? Whales!" shouted Timrod. He ran the portside and saw blowing water coming from the surface.

"Lower my boat, let's go get them," ordered Gerard.

The captain's boat went in alone after the whale pod.

Seeing a giant, old, wrinkled whale alone on the outskirts of the pack, Gerard brought his boat up behind the vulnerable prey.

His harpooner, Timrod, tossed the iron right on its hump behind its blowhole.

The whale pulled Gerard's boat.

"Now take the steering, I'll take him down," said the captain walking to the front with his lance.

Being splashed, and soaked, Gerard picked up the second harpoon hitting it above its left fin. The whale howled like a deep owl or old, sick coyote.

The captain suspected the monster would tire out as it lost more blood. His white shirt began to be stain red.

"Bleed! Bleed you goose and die now!" yelled the angry Captain Gerard, yet the old gray whale continued swimming on with bleeding squirts shooting out of its hump.

"We must let more line out captain!" yelled Timrod. "or he'll drag us under!"

The captain made ready to hit again with his lance.

"Cut his heart, let him be mine!" Gerard said aloud and then stabbed the whale in the right side near his eye.

After a deep growling howl, the whale started to dive.

Gerard loosened the line, making yards and yards of rope drag out.

As the line was getting shorter, the boat crew tied the line on the cleat.

On the other side of the Mako, the boats made to the ship.

"Mr. Tisburn?" yelled Prestern," The captain went a whaling."

"What?" asked Branter.

"The captain put business before his chief mate," said Canonchet, helping him aboard.

Fralhem and his boat crew helped Branter's men while Tisburn watched the captain far off.

"He's got himself a whale," the second mate said. "Ready the sails we'll go after him."

"Fralhem, sir? You're needed on deck," said Connell.

"Wait, Fralhem?" Said Branter. "I'd like to first apologize to Canonchet and you as well, for not listening to you two.

You were right about the storm, and for my ignorance, I call myself an 'ass.'"

"It's alright sir," said Canonchet.

"Yeah, you're not the only one who has done stupid things aboard the ship," said Fralhem. "and we all make mistakes."

On the deck, the active crewmen readied the sails and make for the captain's boat.

"Mr. Fralhem take the wheel as I direct you to Captain Gerard," said Tisburn.

Tisburn and Charlie on the foremast saw Captain

Gerard had himself a giant bull; its tail was longer than the whaleboat, and as it splashed, a wave rocked Gerard's boat up and down.

"No, you don't! You're not pushing me down this time!" yelled Gerard looking as if a red paint had spilled all over him.

"He's ironed a sea giant!" Canonchet said to Tisburn.

The Mako began to catch up with more sails set down, coming up and behind the longboat.

The whaleboat started to slow. "Yes, he's dead now," said, Gerard.

Timrod tossed him the last lance.

In less than a minute, the whale line loosely floated in the waves like a sea snake, and the Nantucket sleigh ride had halted.

The single boat was as still as an autumn leaf floating in a puddle with the dangled line far out and below the sea.

"Come on! Come out, and up from hiding in the blue, and let me turn it all red!" Gerard yelled.

Over 300 yards out, came the old bull, breaching, and splashing out typhoons of water, and blood oozing from its large body.

It dived back in and swam further out. Within seconds the rope ran out and snapped from the cleat, nearly hitting Gerard in the head and scratching his right cheek.

"He's gone, the rope snapped, Captain!" said an oarsman.

"My God he's coming back," said Timrod. The four oarsmen turn to see the old bull charging at them like a steam engine.

Captain Gerard was standing on the front seat of the boat, bleeding from the face but still kept his balance.

"Row me, boys, row me to this bull!" Gerard ordered.

"You shouldn't have come back ya grim wit. I'm going to drive the lance in your eye."

The bull swam straight for them full speed ahead,

Tisburn sides the Mako between the charging whale, and Gerard's boat.

"Grab ahold men; it'll ram into us!" Tisburn ordered.

Charlie hugged the foremast on the lookout nest as he saw the old whale, drive his giant head below the surface, with its flat fluke washing gallons of the ocean on the Mako's deck.

The whale swims under the ship, scratching the keel.

The crew ran to the other side to see the bull breach under the captain's whaleboat, knocking his crew into the ocean, and Gerard flying into the bottom of the ship.

The whale vanished, and the captain's boat crew swam aboard.

When they brought Gerard aboard, he looked like a demon with blood staining his clothes, and face red. The man passed out before he could make an order.

"Take him to his cabin and let's sail out of these waters," said Fralhem returning to the helm.

The crew was in shock at the old, angry whale that had nearly killed their commander. They were even more surprised Gerard was still alive.

CHAPTER 6

PARANOIA

laced on his bunk, alone in his cabin, the Captain twisted and turned in his sleep and sweat rained as his dreams turned to nightmares and sweat rained down from his head.

The nature of the dream was first aboard his ship and on a tropical island. Up top, the lookout spotted an island with a washed-up whale carcass on the white beach. A white seagull pecked at its flesh and sitting on the harpoons sticking out all over its port side.

The crew made him come ashore to butcher the body, but they were later forced to abandon the blubber, due to the hostile Island natives. Back on the ship, the crew turned violent, and the mates tied him up and cast him in the deep tied to the anchor.

As he sank fast below, he could hear the sadist laughter of his crew as the third mate cut the line of the anchor off the ship. As he sat drowning in the depths of the sea, then he awoke.

With a light scream of despair, he sat up from his bunk, banging his forehead on the wooden plank of the bunk, Gerard shook scared and fidgeted like an animal covered in fleas, and his sweat mixed with small tears from his gray eyes.

Looking at his locked door, he saw light shining through the cracks and heard a light knocking.

"Captain Gerard?" came Timrod's voice. "Captain? Is all well in there?"

Gerard jumped from his bunk and grabbed a musket

rifle. "I'm fine!" answered Gerard madly. "Now leave me be!"

The light vanished, and Gerard sat on his deck hugging the musket like a teenager hugging his pillow while sleeping.

"They won't overthrow me," Gerard whispered to himself. "My ship, my ship."

The Mako was headed Southeast, sailing north of the Samoan islands, and south of Tokelau. It was January of 1860, and the Mako's hold still needed to be filled.

Like always Gerard kept to his cabin, only to come out to navigate and steer the ship. He said very little to his crew or mates. Even when they said a kind word like, "Good morning, Captain." Or a friendly "hello," he didn't even look at them.

By mid-January, they found another pod, near the small sand island of Roto.

When closer to the pods, the four boats were lowered and set out for the kill; Gerard's finally took the lead.

Striking into a lone bull, Timrod was handed at lance to slay the beast. While looking out to the other whale spouts, the captain spotted one close to the stern side that was an elder sperm whale. He stared at it in shock when he saw the harpoons sticking from its body; he knew it was the old bull he'd ironed a month back.

Swimming past him, Gerard and his boat watched as the old sperm whale swam off still exposed above the surface.

"Ha! The old bastard lost his guts," said Timrod, with the other men laughing at his joke, although they didn't believe it was the old bull that had almost crushed them only Gerard believed.

With Branter's assistance, towing his kill back to the Mako, Tisburn, and Fralhem remained out for the hunt, coming up from behind like two wolves, and the whale as the deer.

"Here we come, you nursemaid," said Tisburn, with Fralhem's boat to his right.

"Ready yourself mate. Ready your iron, she's coming up," Fralhem ordered.

Tisburn's harpooner was ready along with Canonchet. As its back came close to their view, both harpooners lanced her.

The cow lost more blood and quickly became too weak to keep swimming out. Both boats came up to her, and the two mates drove the long spears into her heart killing her mercilessly.

Below the dead cow, was the young teen calf. It watched helplessly as its mother's life was cut and drained out of her.

The two boats tied the line to her fluke and towed her to the Mako.

As Charlie Evekins broke his back rowing, he and the other rowers could see a small spot of white water shooting in the air.

"Look to your stern Mr. Fralhem." Said Charlie, "we're being followed."

The mate turned and saw the calf whale, just about the size of the boat, trailing right behind the cow's dead body.

Fralhem knew it had to be the cow's infant; he turned to Charlie who had the same look of sadness and regret in his eyes.

"This is a cruel business Charlie," said Fralhem sitting next to the tiller.

"Sometimes I think it's the poor whale that has suffered worse than us."

"Me too, sir," said Evekins. "The poor creature."

Setting the two whales on each side of the vessel, the

men work non-stop cutting and boiling the whale's flesh into the burning oil. And out from the bottom of the female whale, sharks scattered, as the young calf swam around making sad moans as it watched the slaughter of its mother.

Fralhem's men had been quiet the whole time, not singing or laughing at Tisburn's jokes, ever since Charlie had told them that they had slain a mother whale. The men stayed quiet, regrets running through their minds.

After they had washed and readied for sleep, they kneeled and prayed to God for forgiveness, and the best for the poor orphan calf, they had created.

It was now a year from home, and the Mako continued the slaughter of the leviathans, now at a half-full hold, yet the captain still made no impression on his crew, and they saw him still carrying weapons. Worse even, Prestern informed the officers, that Gerard paid Timrod a dollar to taste his food for him before eating.

It was now evident in Branter's mind the captain was as paranoid as a mad king. He still told Tisburn, and Fralhem keeps his orders and again make the best of it although they were now afraid to even knock on the Captain's door.

CHAPTER 7

A Beached Kill

In mid-February 1860, the Mako was now sailing south-west of the Niue islands.

Below deck Prestern reported to Branter that most of the freshwater barrels were leaking. When the word reached the crew, they demanded the officers make for land to fix them.

The first mate knew he had to get the go-ahead from the captain, so he went below taps on his door.

There was no answer any so Branter knocked more loudly. "Captain Gerard?" he called, opening the door that was unlocked. The mate peeked through. The cabin was dark, but from the light shining through the stern window, he saw Gerard with half his body sleeping on his deck, with two pistols grabbed in his hands.

The chief mate walked to Gerard's side and shrugged his shoulder.

The captain sat up. "What?! What then?! Oh, Mr. Branter," said Gerard lowering his weapons, "What is it?!" Informing the captain of the leaking water supplies, Gerard, ordered to have the carpenter tar them. Branter repeated that the crew had insisted they make for land.

The captain cared not for what the men were thinking, yet he did not want to anger his crew some more.

"Oh, very well," said Gerard. "We'll make for Levuka. But tell me this, my lieutenant, if I do this will the men be happy with this?"

"I'm sure they'll be grateful to stretch their legs, and not fear as a tyrant," answered Branter.

The Mako made it to the Fiji Isles, inhabited with both European merchants and mostly hostile native, the thing whalers always try to avoid. They passed by the small deserted jungle islands that could have fresh water in ponds or stream, but they fear the islands are the reservations for the savage cannibals, so the whalers ignored them and made for Ovalau, to the port town of Levuka.

On a warm morning, while passing more tiny islands, the lookout spotted something huge, washing along the white beach line.

The mates and the captain looked to the starboard to where the island.

"Ja I see it!" said Fralhem, passing the watch scope to Tisburn.

"It's a beached whale, and it's a monster," said the 2cd mate. "Must be an 80-footer, 15 tons of it."

When the First mate looked through it and saw its large body was flopping around in the tide.

"I can see the gulls are enjoying that beast's flesh; perhaps we should collect its blubber before it rots?" Aye Captain?" the mate asked handing Gerard the scope.

The captain didn't answer, nor looked through the glass, but stared off into space. The captain had a blank expression; He remembered the nightmare he'd had that had led to his death, to him it was an omen. The crew insisted on going to shore to collect the flesh of a dead whale. His paranoia and anxieties fought out in his mind, making his head throb.

"I… I must let them go! They'll think I'm going mad if I don't!" Gerard said out loud.

"What's that sir?" said Branter, shaken by the shouting.

"I huh… Nothing! Nothing!" answered Gerard.

"I'm not sure it's a clever idea, the island might have savages inhabiting it."

"How about we use them rifles in your cabin?" asked Fralhem. "We can go hunting for hogs if it has any."

"Yeah, be nice to have meat with our fresh island water and fruit," said Tisburn.

The captain saw his crew behind looking at the island crewmen had their eyes on him.

"Alright go on, but make back for the ship before dusk," said Captain Gerard.

The nervous crew, now happy at finally stepping on land after over a year at sea, we're going to butcher a beached whale, they had not harpooned. It looked to be an easy job for them, and their fear of hostile cannibals disappeared since the captain had the lack of courage only to supply his men with limited firearms.

Four boats went to the island with most of the crew, over 27 men, while Captain Gerard stayed aboard with just the two-remaining ship-keepers.

CHAPTER 8

A Peeking Party

The boats made it to the beaches with some of the crew jumping off to hug the dry sandy beach, including Charlie Evekins.

The crew brought along cutting tools like boarding knives, blubber pikes, and hooks to peel off the whale blubber, only six muskets and a dozen empty barrels mostly for the water but also for the whale blubber.

The hunting party of Tisburn, Fralhem, Canonchet, Sam Witty, Owen Sween, Tom Prestern and Charlie Evekins armed with muskets. Their job was to go out to collect the water and fruit, and if lucky to hunt hogs.

Branter was to stay on the beach, with the 20 other men to cut the blubber off the dead whale. Most of the hunting party had the firearms, and only Branter had a single pistol, but the crew had no worries.

But back aboard the Mako, Captain Gerard was thinking about how that dream was coming true with the beached whale and his crew, but he calmed himself by realizing he hadn't gone ashore to help and he spent hours wandering the deck to trying to let go of the nightmare and his worries. He went back to his cabin to sip some grog he kept aboard for himself.

In the jungle, both Tisburn, and Fralhem armed with rifles took the lead, as Evekins, Sween, and Witty hauled the five large empty barrels that would soon be heavier with drinking water.

Canonchet led the way as the scout, hiking in on the

moist, humid land, under the dark shaded of the thick jungle leaves.

Canonchet came yelling, “Tisburn! Fralhem! Found water!”

Prestern and the two mates ran ahead in excitement to see the large clear pond connected to a narrow stream with clean running water.

Back on the beach, the white sand had become red with the streams of whale blood. They cut off large flesh chunks and the harpooner Mr. Timrod brought the cut blubber strips back aboard the ship to be boiled.

While the butchery continued, Branter sent a sailor to collect some coconuts. The man walks from the beach to the foot of the dark jungle.

He looks to a palm tree and saw some fresh coconuts had already fallen, so he knelt to pick one up. When he kneeled to pick one up he thought he had seen something hanging... and it was not a leaf, but a branch with a decaying corpse hanging like a sick decoration.

The sailor dropped the coconut, as he could hear whispers and rustles in the jungle and knew they weren’t friendly tones, but an ambush. He ran off back to the whale carcass.

Back in the jungle, the hunting party used the running stream waterfall to fill the barrels, using buckets. While doing it, they heard funny sounds and splashes.

All the six hunters went to investigate the noise.

Hiding behind bushes, then men spot a group of native women bathing in the pond.

All the six whalers were aroused, and their jaws dropped as they stared at the naked island ladies.

On the beach, Branter saw the sailor running along with his arms waving in the air. He heard his panic cry.

“Run to the boat! To the boats!” yelled the crewmen,

making the rest stop cutting the whale and looking up at the frightened crewmen. "Cannibals!"

After yelling that, dozens of natives with white war paint on their faces sprinted out from the jungle line onto the beach, wielding long spears, and hatchets.

"To the boats!" yelled Branter. "Back to the ship!"

The whaler's eyes were bright with fear; they jumped off the dead whale. Some got into the boats, and others started to take off swimming to the ship.

Mr. Branter the only beach crewmen armed with a musket, fired off a shot, hitting one charging cannibal.

The shot was heard far to the Mako and into the jungle.

"Gunshot?" said Fralhem, "a nein."

The whalers stopped peeking at the naked island girls and ran to the barrels.

"Maybe it's a warning or a signal." Said Canonchet.

"Stand by Mr. Fralhem," said Tisburn. "Prestern,

Evekins and I will take a look. Fill the barrels, meet us at the beach and stay alert."

Charlie followed Tisburn, and Prestern to the beach.

Fralhem looked to see some of the bathing native girls leaving the swimming hole and realized something was up.

"Let's fills these barrels quickly." He said. "I think there's trouble afoot."

The beach crew made off the beach into the sea swimming to the boats fleeing to the Mako, but Mr. Branter who tried to reload for a second shot was overrun. The man tried to fight back using the musket as a bat.

But he was hopelessly outnumbered as nearly a hundred mad cannibals tackled him. A blunt hit to his head knocked the first mate unconscious.

The last thing the mate herd before losing his senses were gunshots.

CHAPTER 9

Fire Fight

Tisburn, Prestern, and Evekins hurried out to the beach and spotted the large war party of natives carrying the first mate Branter away.

Prestern opened fire, as did the second mate, killing two natives, the war band charged the trio of intruders.

"We need to get off this island!" shouted Prestern dropping his gun and began running to the sea.

Tisburn reloaded and saw Evekins staring with a blank stare.

"What are you waiting for you idiot, shoot! Shoot!"

Tisburn yelled out as he was hit by a flying spear that was thrown by the natives. The sharp wooden spear cut into the mate's upper shoulder, making him drop the musket, and shout in pain.

Charlie grabbed the mate and helped him into the water.

"Swim Mr. Tisburn," said Charlie, "you must make for the ship."

As Tisburn runs in and swims off. The natives took Charlie.

Tisburn turned and saw Evekins being captured by the savages.

With Prestern's help, the second mate made it aboard the Mako.

The crew was in shock and close to a violent breakdown.

They shouted questions at him in panic, "Where're the other officers?" Are they dead? They're gonna eat them!" and some asked.

"What are we gonna do Mr. Tisburn?"

Hearing that the mate made for the captain's quarters, with his hand restraining his wound.

Barging through he saw that Captain Gerard had got himself drunk, and asleep on his chair.

Disappointed, and anger with his careless, stupid superior he ordered Timrod, and Prestern to take out more muskets and pistols from the captain's closet.

Of his own volition, Tisburn ordered a rescue party to the island, as soon as Connell patched his bleeding wound.

When over half the crew were armed and walked around the deck with loaded weapons, the rest held swords, the intoxicated captain climbed out from the hull on deck and saw his armed crew.

Gerard's fears had built up in his drunken brain and thought the dream had come true, and his crew was going to mutiny.

"No, I knew it," he stated to himself. "The dream is my future; they will kill me!"

Some of the crew noticed captain Gerard's mad rant, as he ran back down the deck back in his cabin.

"I think the dandy Captain has gone off his wits," a sailor said to Timrod as he polished a pistol.

Tisburn just rolled his eyes as his wounded was all stitched up.

"Now to the boats and let's save our shipmates," the second mate ordered.

Back on the island right in the middle of the jungle was the cannibal encampment. Here the huts were decorated with skulls and bones, and there were fire spits with half-naked natives shouting, chanting and playing drums around the flames.

"Oh Mr. Branter wake up man, you must get up,"

said Charlie Evekins who was tied across from him on a grounded pole. "Mr. Branter you must escape. Otherwise, we're all done for, the whole Mako crew and us as well."

But the mate didn't respond. Two cannibals came up to the two prisoners, but Charlie could not understand the language the natives were speaking, and he tried to plea for his officer's life.

They cut Charlie and brought him and Branter up to a pair chopping blocks.

The bare wooden logs had stains of human blood on them and a human skull tied around the mass.

And up in front of the blocks was a roasting spit atop of a blazing roaring fire.

Charlie's heart was pounding in fear deep in his chest and a tear dripped out of his eye.

They put him down on his knees and placed his head on the chop, on his side, he could see the knocked-out mate placed beside him.

With a barefoot pushing their backs down, two tribesmen came up behind them with long sharp blades they must have traded or stolen from other sailors, to behead them.

Charlie felt the sharp blade touch the back of his next as the executioners lined up the strike.

The two cannibals lifted the sabers in the air over their heads. Charlie Evekins closed his eyes and took a deep breath; guns shots came to his hearing.

Evekins hears the crowd of natives screaming in panic.

He opened his eyes and saw the two-armed cannibals had been shot dead.

Sitting up, he saw two other cannibals shot dead.

He turned to the source of gunfire and saw his savors.

"Fralhem!" Charlie yelled. "Good Mr. Fralhem!"

It was, Fralhem, Canonchet, Witty, and Sween who came out of the jungle.

Which way are we going again?" Sween Asked.

"Anywhere but here, just run straight for the coast," answered Fralhem.

They ran at lantern point away from the encampment,

With Fralhem guarding Canonchet who was carrying Branter. The whalers could hear the natives shout, and yell from behind; they knew they're being hunted in hot pursuit.

"Run men!" said Witty, "don't stop, keep moving!"

Running past shrubs, jumping fallen trees, and splashing in puddles, the six men made it to the beach.

"Now what Fralhem?" asked Sween. "How do we get off this island?"

"We have to find the ship," the third mate answered.

"They can't have left us."

Now running down the beach, the men removed their shoes to help them run faster on the sand. Making go distances, it was more than two minutes when the cannibal hunting warriors charged out after them.

It was now near dawn with the sun cracking over the east. The men kept running until they could see their ship.

"Oh, thank Christ!" shouted Sween, "They didn't leave us."

"More to thank God for it looks like boats are coming" said Canonchet getting tired from running and carrying them first mate.

"Alright then let's make for them, and get off this spit of land" said Fralhem.

Swimming into the sea off the beach they made for the coming boats.

On the whaleboats, the sailor on the bow seat spotted the coming swimmers.

“Mr. Tisburn?!” Jeth the cabin boy shouted. “It’s them Fralhem, and the others.”

Tisburn made the boats pick them up.

“Bring them in let’s leave this savage island,” the second mate ordered.

“What of the beached whale?” asked Timrod.

“Leave it. To hell with that beast; it can rot away for the savages to pick off,” answered Tisburn, bringing his mate Branter aboard.

CHAPTER 10

Hospital in The Steering

On the ship's quarterdeck, Branter was taken below. The first mate made noises as if struggling to awake, but Tisburn and Fralhem wanted him in the best care.

"Charlie? Canonchet? Fetch Prestern to prepare a meal for yourselves," said Fralhem. "Witty? Have all shipmates turn over the firearms."

"Aye, but I think it's best for us officers to control the guns," said Tisburn. "I'm afraid Captain Gerard is really losing it; the fool got himself drunk, locked himself in his cabin like always where he hoarded the rum for himself and the weapons."

The two mates looked down the stairway that led to the captain's room. They could see Gerard's passed out body lying at the foot of the steps.

"Pitiful, absolutely pitiful," said Fralhem. The third mate stepped over the drunk captain and brought up a bottle of grog.

"Let's take the ship to Levuka," said Tisburn. "Hate to admit but it but the captain was right about the cannibals.

We should wait till Branter recovers and we'll make him captain."

"Yeah, maybe Gerard knew cannibals were inhabiting that island," said Fralhem. "And as he didn't give us enough muskets to fight them off, he did not care about us."

"Aye, but with Branter's a head injury, we still have to wait," said Tisburn.

"Well, we should keep a good watch on him," said Fralhem "and if that captain touches him, he's a dead man."

His eyes closed but ears wide open, the captain had awakened after Fralhem stepped over. He listened through the mate's conversation about his removal and placing Branter in charge.

Above he heard Tisburn, and Fralhem were piloting the vessel and Canonchet, Evekins, Jethro and Prestern tending the ill Branter. He was being kept under the protective eye from Gerard, so he's not able to kill him. It was now apparent to the crew that their unstable captain wanted the officers dead.

Two days after leaving the cannibal island, the Mako arrived at the civilized trading island of Ovalau. Most of the crew had recovered, including Branter, who had gained all consciousness but was still down, due to a fever.

Branter was laid on a warm stretcher and placed on a soft beach as the whalers traded with the peaceful locals, British, and Dutch merchants.

The crew made exchanges with their oil for fresh food, meat, fruits, and vegetables. More importantly Fralhem, and Tisburn purchase medicines and spices from the East Indian trade merchants to help with the first mate's illness.

The day was like a holiday picnic with the crew roasting chicken and lamb over a fire pit by the beach, enjoying music from the island natives and some crewmen traded scrimshaw for gifts to bring home to their loved ones.

It was now the third day off the coast, it was time to leave, and Captain Gerard ordered to make course south-east.

Later that night. Evekins awoke to a strange racket.

Getting out of his bunk he saw cabin boy Jeth, with his coat on and his hammock sack containing his belonging.

The kid made his way to the steps on deck, and Evekins followed as the rest of the crew slept.

Evekins saw Jeth take a lifebuoy from the try-works, then made for the side facing the land.

It was clear he was deserting the ship.

The sailor came up from behind the young boy, with a light hand on his shoulder.

"Jet? Jeth?" asked Charlie. "Where are you off?"

"Oh, I'm off this voyage," answered Jethro looking to the full moon. "And off on other adventures."

"Well, don't you think your mother will be expecting you to come home, as she sees your ship on that Montauk beach?" asked Evekins.

Jeth looked down to the deck.

"I have no mother or a home," Jethro said. "I go to sea, jump vessel to vessel continent to continent. I'm going to see the rest of the world in all the oceans; please don't stop me."

Charlie saw how the brave young lad looked so serious.

Although Charlie, he too had no one back home to go back either, he felt he must stay, but let Jethro go off.

"Well, I wish nothing but the best of luck in all the world for you, friend," said Charlie, his hand to the boy. Jethro shook it and with Charlie's help, climbed down into the water on the buoy, and the cabin boy made his way to land, deserting the Mako.

"Good lad, you'll make a great man," Charlie said to himself. "Take care, Jethro."

"Ah making for land?" Charlie jumped "Abandoning ship?" said Fralhem coming from behind him.

Charlie was frightened that he would be punished for helping a deserter.

"I did something like that when I was his age," Fralhem said lighting up his pipe.

"Real…really? You jumped off a ship?" Said Charlie, when he realized the mate was not going to punish him.

"Well sort of similar," said Fralhem. "I never deserted a whaleship, I deserted my home, and… and… family."

"You abandoned your own family?" asked Charlie in shock.

"No…no not like… Ah Never mind!" Said Fralhem who began mumbling in Norwegian.

"No sir, you can tell me, we're shipmates," Charlie said, running in front of him. "Why did you leave your country?"

Looking into the eyes from the light of the pipe, Charlie could see Fralhem, had a tear in his eye, but Fralhem agreed to tell him and brought the sailor to the Alf deck near the helm piloting the vessel.

CHAPTER 11

From Mountains to Sea

Charlie Evekins had been an open book aboard the Mako, telling the mates, Perstern, Sween, Witty, Connell, and Jethro of his life as a homeless orphan on the streets of Salem. He never knew his father and his mother left him as a child. When he turned 13, he drifted from Boston, around Cape Cod, stowing away on a wagon to New Bedford, where he had fallen in love with ships. How back in the orphanage he read aloud to other children of sea tales, and most of all stories of whaling. Now five years later, at 18 he had signed on to the Mako of Nantucket, and that was his life.

Now he was to learn the story of his third mate Fralhem.

After a view puffs of the corn pipe, the mate began his story.

"I was never born a sea-goer, but a wood cutting landsman, and I was not given the name Fralhem. I was born Vilhelm Membjorg, to a Sami logger and a Danish farm girl. In my early youth as a six-year-old, I started manual labor… well minor labor, like fetching tools, and meals for the lumber mill workers, and stacking up piles of firewood for our neighbors. Not quite a fun childhood for me.

Times when I learned at a real early age of work and earning, my father always made sure I was given a wage, yet still made sure a whip of his belt punished me if I slacked off chores or came home empty-handed.

"On my first log drive down a river, we had taken cut timber down a river to a Swedish port, where we sold the logs and the timber to be built into hulls and docks.

When we arrived at a port in Sweden it was the very first time I've ever seen a full-rigged ship docked in the harbor, I also saw many warships, schooners, and sloops and they were beautiful. I said to myself, 'What have I been missing?' It was love at first sight. I wanted to go to sea, on a ship.

When I shared my dream with my father, he said 'You are never to be a sailor, you will not go to sea.'

His tone was angry, yet I was a child who was dominated by his parents and was always obedient.

It was on a journey north back to Norway, in the icy river, late in the night when our longboat was capsized, by a lone drift log. It lifted us right under the water pushing us up like it was the finger of the Devil flipping us.

I nearly drowned in my heavy wool clothes, in the pitch-dark night, but my hand held onto a rope tied to the Boat. I pulled my massive wet form on the flopped boat, while other woodsmen hung on to the boat, I heard others that couldn't swim scream and shout like infants, and I remembered one of whom yelled my very name.

"Vilhelm!" and it was the voice of my father.

That morning we five out of eight kicked the boat to the land we made it back safely, but my father was missing.

I ran up and down the side of the river bank screaming out the top of my lungs. "Papa! Papa!" And then my fellow loggers had found him… dead.

His body had washed to the shore, and when I was informed he was dead, I fainted.

I awoke on my bed in my family's cabin. As I stood I heard, my pregnant mother sobbing on her knees in front of the fireplace, and a newly buried grave was right outside of our home.

I was now responsible in looking after my mum and

our home by giving her as much care as I could for as long as possible.

I cooked and served food, keeping the place warm, giving her medicine and staying by her side every night. I cleaned the floor, swept, dusted neighbor cabins and warehouses, and shoveled snow to buy clothes for my coming sibling.

Finally, mother gave birth, I got her help from the local midwife, and that evening my little brother Kristopher was born. I never saw her so happy as the second child was placed in her arms. And I joined her in sleeping with the newborn.

Yet the happy, loving moments were not to last. Mother became so ill with a fever and my brother and I were taken away as she laid dying in the bed of what was supposed to be a family home. Mother past two weeks after the birth of Kristopher and we were now orphaned.

After a year of living in an orphanage in Stavanger, I did it,

I ran away, leaving what was left of my only family behind in the care of the orphan keepers, to go sailing.

I was seven at the time. I started in net fishing and then at the age of ten, I served a voyage on a merchant ship, sailing to Canada and Greenland.

Finally, when I was 13, I went whaling.

"On the Ericsson?" asked Charlie.

"The Eriksson, of Tonsberg, with a k," Fralhem corrected.

She was not like this Nantucket ship, of three masts and fully rigged with whaleboats.

The Eriksson was like our great Viking longships of 40-foot-long, single mast, square sail with a crew of 18 men. 16 of us sailors would do the rowing and deck-work as our captain manned the rudder on the stern while the last man stood at the bow handling the harpoons.

Unlike the American whalers that slaughter the whales for oil and profit, we hunted for their meat; mostly minks, and bowheads.

I was 15 when I had slain my first whale; it was an event so unforgettable and I was almost lost on another capsized boat.

Fralhem paused after, and emptied his pipe, stood up and began to walk off.

"What happened with that first whale?" asked Charlie.

Fralhem walked up to the bow deck with his face down.

"Another time right now stay with the helm.

The third mate relaxed his elbows on the foredeck railing with his hand covering his face. Charlie stared at the man knowing; he had to be lost in sad feelings of the loss of parents, his abandoned sibling, and all tragic events that happened in his past. All of that went around Charlie Evekin's mind as the sun began to rise.

CHAPTER 12

A Step-Down

The vessel was now headed toward the whaling ground near the Cook Islands where rights and sperm whales would be migrating.

A week passed before the crew, and Gerard realized the cabin boy had deserted the voyage, but they all had little concern or care.

When Evekins gave the word, they accepted the boy's departure, to go around the world freely, while they all stayed loyal in the dangerous business, under a tyrant bully of a captain.

Branter was quite sad for he'd always had the cabin boy aboard his whaleboat and he reminded him of his son, back in New Bedford.

It was not uncommon, for a crew member to desert the whale ship voyage; it was no great surprise for someone to flee along dangerous job that made little profits for himself.

So, the whaleship Mako carried on with the long voyage.

Morale of the crew was neither angry since the hull was now nearing full of oil, but nor cheerful since the departure of the cabin boy.

On the deck, the crew tended their daily ship chores.

With only Gerard crying out the orders as if he was an officer.

"Where the hell are those idiots?" Gerard asked himself.

Where were Tisburn and Fralhem to shout out his commands?

Why were they not on the deck hearing is words?

Leaving Mr. Timrod to the steering, Gerard searched for the mates.

"Mr. Branter?" Asked The captain coming into the officer's cabin, only to find it abandoned and Branter's bunk empty with his sheets hanging off the side.

"Where are you twits?!" Gerard yelled. Below deck with no one there the crew's quarters in forecastle was all empty of men.

Gerard began to think his officers were fooling with him until a spot of light with coming from the hatch leading far down to the oil barrel hold and he figured that the mates were down there.

Far below in the hold surrounded by black barrels, with lanterns as the sores of light, where the three officers were having a private meeting.

"Now I'm afraid Fralhem is right," said Tisburn. "Gerard it too careless, arrogant and too incompetent to captain us."

"See Mr. Branter?" Fralhem asked. "It's time to make you the ship's master, and we need to make Gerard step down."

Coughing with a wet cloth around his head, Branter finally agreed.

"Yes, I suppose you're right," said the first mate. "He hoards all the weapons and grog gets himself drunk and does not act like a professional leader."

"Yet it will be trouble," Fralhem said holding the lit lamp. "Once we finish this voyage, and return for the owners to discover we've mutinied, could place us all in an awful lot of trouble."

"Yeah might be a killing ground we'll be walking upon," said Tisburn.

"Leave that to me shipmates, I doubt he'll ever get a rope around us," said Branter when the three mates heard the clicking of pistol hammers, they turned and saw Gerard pointing his pistols at them.

"Oh yes, my father will be sure to have you lot hanged if you so much as stand against me," said Gerard shaking his flintlocks. "I should put an end to you all right now.

Bad idea sir," said Tisburn, before Fralhem interrupted.

"Oh yes more mistakes a stupid mindless fool would make!" said Fralhem slowly walking up to the young, shaken captain. "You know Captain Gerard, it's true we are standing against yee; you're too young and arrogant to be captain, and it was your rich papa who gave you this rank. Your pop can't kill us; he may be a ship owner, and well connected, but so is Branter.

His father-in-law a state senator so we know powerful people too.

So now you hear our proposal to step down as captain, give those pistols to us, and when this hunting voyage ends, we return to Nantucket and rid ourselves of each other's company afterward and we'll never see one another again."

Fralhem came real close holding the lamp up in between the pistols and his face, with sweaty, shaking Gerard now pinned up against a wall of oil barrels.

"I…I… I can kill you right now," said Gerard still holding to two pistols at Fralhem.

"No, you won't, tosk," said Fralhem. "Kill us, officers, and the crew will cast you off the ship, or if you shoot me now, I drop this lamp, and this whole ship will blow up like a floating volcano, and you'll be one of the first to die, so don't even ask me to put it down. Now hand over the pistols or me drop this lamp."

A pink-faced Gerard lost his grip on the guns and them dropped on the floor.

“Thank you, Captain,” said Branter picking up the two weapons.

“Let’s get back on deck.”

“Yeah let’s finish this hunt as real whalers,” said Tisburn.

“I knew he’d do it,” said Fralhem, putting out the light, leaving Gerard sobbing like an infant cuddled against the foul-smelling barrels, no longer in full command of the Mako.

CHAPTER 13

Hauled Away

Hundreds of sea miles south-west of Mangaia Island, dozens of whale pods, were now in sight, enough to fill the Mako's hull.

On the first day, they arrived in the South Cook island waters, the cry of "Thar she blows!"

Four boats were lowered, and the Mako crew killed of whales, two a day.

Late in April, the hull was now near full, having 1900 full barrels of oil and the sperm whales were still in the grasp of the hunters. That day Branter ordered two boats to take both sides of the ship separately to go after them.

Gerard and Tisburn went to the starboard, while Branter and Fralhem took the port. Before the hunt, the second and third mate made a bet on which man would slay the last whale for this voyage. So Fralhem was going to do his hunting spree to the far level, ordered Canonchet to strike any whale that reaches his boat and push his boatmen to pull faster.

In Fralhem's boat were seven men; an extra rower like before with harpooner Mat Canonchet, old Tom Prestern,

Kevin Connell, Owen Sween, Sam Witty, and Charlie Evekins.

The fourth boat by past Branter's boat, with its crew shouting, "Cheater! Cheater!"

"Uh ignore them boys, were beating Branter, let's beat Tisburn, and win ourselves $50. I'll share with you all!"

"Ready up Canny! Ready yourself, I see a big one ahead it's breaching!"

Hearing the order, the harpoon warrior stood up and saw a baby calf swimming with the mother.

"Hit it Canny! strike her!" yelled Fralhem, and with a swift push, the harpoon flawed straight through the water like a thunderbolt and into the female's back.

"Oars in, and let the line go out," said Fralhem. "She'll tire herself.

The line was yanked out by the yards, and the rope pile began to get smaller, as Witty and Evekins slowed the line up using thick mittens, Prestern tied the line to the cleat and off went the whaleboat.

Bearing fast into the wind direction, the longboat flopped up and down from the tide waves made by the cow's fluke shadowed by her calf.

The female swam at a panicked speed making her young swim farther ahead.

From between the long whaleboat and the frightened female came the orphaned calf. The young sperm whale madly waved his tail, coming up fast to the harpoon line.

The seven whalers on the boat spotted the 30ft whale. It jumped out from the surface and dove back under, unknown to them were two things.

The young bull took the rope in his jaw and with its big teeth cut the mother whale free and pulled the whaleboat in a different direction. The mother whale and her calf swam off while the orphan calf hauled the boat away.

"Fralhem!?" yelled Charlie. "Did you see that? It cut us away from her."

"No way! That's nonsense," said Fralhem.

"I lost my harpoon," said Canonchet." The little bull snapped the line, and now it's hauling us."

The rest of the men looked to one another; they couldn't believe the single young whale was strategic enough to save a strang whale and lead them away from the big kill. The most dumbfounded was the mate Fralhem, for in his career he had never seen a whale do this before.

The whale was unharmed, and its mouth closed in on the line as it kept pulling the 24-foot long whaleboat fast out into the South Pacific.

"Mr. Fralhem we ought to cut it loose," said Connell.

"Nah," replied the mate. "We'll slay that little bastard when he tires."

"Uh sir I think you should cut loose," said Charlie, because he out of all the other whalers, had noticed the second most important thing. "Because I can't see the Mako anywhere."

All the whalers looked at him and to the stern of the boat where the ship was always located when they were out hunting, yet the ship was nowhere to be seen.

"What? What?!" Fralhem looked back hoping Charlie was joking, but one good glimpse behind he couldn't find the ship.

"Cut it loose Canny," Fralhem ordered.

The Pequot took out his Bowie knife, and with one chop the rope was gone. The boat slowly halted out in the open sea.

The seven men looked in every direction, all blue, from the top light sky, and bottom dark wavy ocean.

"Oh no! lordy no, where's the damn ship?!" yelled out Witty.

"The little beast hauled us out in the middle of nowhere," said, Sween.

"No! Don't panic boys," said Fralhem. "We'll find the ship."

The mate took from his pocket a compass, pointing northward to the opposite direction where his boat went out.

The officer had the men put the oars back in the water, to row back. The sky had not a single cloud. The hot sun beat down on the oarsmen. All were dressed in trousers and long-sleeved shirts. Four men including Charlie had no hats on so he tore fabrics from his sleeves and make them into cowls from Witty's sewing kit, for him, and old Prestern.

Canonchet shared his hat with Connell, and Witty needed no cap since his bushy hair covered it well, like Canonchet's long, black locks.

Their long hair and sleeves protected their skin from sunburn, yet they sweated like fat farm hogs, and wet stains came through their chest, back, and armpit areas.

Fralhem looked out to the north horizon, searching in every corner, looking out for their missing vessel.

Dozens of whale spouts and flukes were spotted, and they had not a concern but for their survival. They abandoned the whale hunt to find their ship.

Nothing, hour by hour passed by, and the sun began to set.

The men start to grow weak from the rowing, and Fralhem's arm began to lose nerve; he stood up to look around and tried to get the circulation back in his numb limb.

The sailors had no watch, so they did not know the exact time of the day.

"Alright boy stop, stop the rowing, and rest up," said Fralhem plumbing back down on the stern seat. The men drop the oars with a big tired moan and grunts.

"Any sign of the ship? Sir?" asked Canonchet.

"Hope...hopefully in the morning," answered Fralhem.

All the boat crew had hundreds of questions and worries

about their situation, yet they were so tired they dropped to the boat's floor to fall asleep.

Only the mate stayed awake with a glowing lantern on a pole hooks. The seven men were lost on that morning of April the 21st 1860.

CHAPTER 14

In A Situation

On the afternoon of the 21st, Charlie saw Fralhem stand up on the middle of his seat with his spyglass, scanning every area out into the open water.

"Any sign of the Mako?" asked Charlie seeing the rest of the men awake.

The other men shook their heads. On every side of the whaleboat they spotted only whale spouts blowing, tails splashing, and small shark fins circling the boat.

"What are we to do sir?" asked Charlie. "Where do we go?"

"Nowhere," answered Sween. "There's nowhere to go; we're far into the center of Oceania. We're lost!"

"Stop! We are not lost," said Fralhem. "Branter will look for us."

'You got us into this Fralhem, said Connell. "If we are not found wh…"

"Then I'll get you all out of this!" Fralhem interrupted. Even if I must lay down my own life. Now cut the blaming, and let's stay calm, we'll make it out of this."

The second day of losing sight of the vessel passed like the first. And the tension of the sailors grew with more panic and anger.

"Oh God where's the ship?!" yelled Connell. "No whaleboats, sails, nothing!"

"Stay seated Mr. Connell!" said Fralhem.

"You got us into the…" said Owen began.

"I know! Shut up!" yelled Fralhem real ticked off.

"Just shut up I said I'll get us out of this, now all of you hand me your belongings."

The men looked to one another, but they followed the order, and emptied their belts and side arms.

Fralhem emptied his pockets and revealed a 10" fillet knife and a sack of gunpowder.

Canonchet had his knife, Striker set, and three fishing hooks.

Charlie had only a pocket knife.

Connell, the carpenter, had his whiskey flask, small steel hammer, a dozen nails, and measuring tape.

Witty had his sewing kit with thread, needles, a small reflecting mirror and a shaving razor.

Prestern had a box of matches, four hard tack biscuits, a gray rag, and his pipe but no tobacco.

Sween, had his own compass, spare eyeglasses, blank papers, three writing pens, and two small books of Edgar Allen Poe's, Arthur Gordon Pym's narrative, and a small global atlas.

"Alright, each of your items will be our survival kit; same with the gear on this boat. We'll use the oars as the mast and turn our tarpaulin into a sail." Fralhem ordered. "And with Mr. Sween's atlas, and two compasses we will make it."

"What of food and fresh water?" asked Connell. "The four biscuits won't last."

"I'm aware of that," Fralhem said annoyed by Connell's unhelpful comments.

"We'll fish," said Canonchet. "And there's a small barrel of fresh water, under Fralhem's seat."

"Or eat each other," Sween said to Connell who nodded in agreement.

"Oh, for the love of God, shut up!" Yelled Fralhem.

"Negative thinking will be your death, keep your minds positive and let's work to get out of this."

"Yeah you heard the man, let's set sail," said Charlie.

Late on the second day before sunset, the boat crew made a single mast, with a long rigging, made by Connell.

Canonchet and Witty turned the white oval shaped tarp into a triangular lateen sail. The second night had weak wind, and the boat barely moved.

The men looked to the rear of the boat seeing Fralhem reading Sween's atlas book by lantern light.

"So, Mr. Fralhem, you have any idea which way we're heading?" asked Connell, lying cross-legged in the boat.

"I'll tell you all in the morning get some rest," Said Fralhem.

"You know, don't be so hard on him," Charlie said to Connell. "I'm sure he'll do what he can for our survival."

"Let's hope to God you're right," replied Connell. "hope and pray every night."

The boat crew sat down in the boat under their blank seats, with their shirts, rolled into pillows to rest their head as they tried to get comfortable in the rocking boat, some were too tired to think while others had deep worries on what lies ahead in this voyage.

CHAPTER 15

IN THE MIDDLE OF A WHALE SCHOOL

So west it was. Fralhem made a course to the nearest land, where the trade wind made a fast breeze for the small whaleboat made into a tiny sloop.

The Mako was right in between the Cook and Tonga Isles. Fralhem chose Tonga, less than 500 miles west of their position.

"Why westward?" asked Sween. "The winds are making a north breeze, we can catch Niue, and the Tongas might have cannibals."

Fralhem just steered the tiller and looked out to the blue sea line but answered.

"It's either a singular island that we could bypass into more open ocean, or a group of isles we could run into, to supply ourselves with the previsions the land can offer."

"What about cannibals?" asked Witty.

"Let's not worry about that now," said Fralhem. "Let's just make for land."

Prestern, Canonchet, and Charlie had their confidence in the mate, but Connell, Sween, and even Witty still had grave doubts, and again blamed their mate.

As they sailed on, Fralhem broke one of Prestern's large hard biscuits into pieces of six, as their only midday ration, and gave them each a single dipper full of water.

Canonchet started to ready the fishing line using Witty's

thread and his hooks. He then cut his thumb to douse his blood on a cloth and hooked it on for the fish to smell the bait.

By the third day, there was still no fish, only more and more spouts from the sperm whale pod.

From a small distance away, the men saw whales on all sides of the boat.

"Still can't see why a young calf whale pulled us so fast and so far away from our ship," said Charlie.

"Because it didn't!" said Fralhem. "We rowed too far out, the female pulled a near mile of rope, and the calf then came out of nowhere, and it snapped it. Whales aren't that persuasive, or clever in the brain; they're just animals."

"Will the Mako search for us? Sir?" asked Prestern.

"I'm sure Branter noticed we didn't return from the hunt and saw us being dragged off. He's probably looking for us right now, sweeping the whole area, I'm sure of it."

"What if he gives us up?" asked Sween. "And leave us behind?"

"That's something Gerard would do," answered Fralhem.

"Branter's an honorable man." The six men shook heads in agreement.

"Yet we're going the other way," said Sween. "What if the search is right back where we were?" he said pointing back.

"I can't be sure, or guarantee it," Fralhem said. "They might be searching the wrong way; worry not, there are other whalers sailing these waters, so we just carry on."

On the boat, they sat in their usual crew positions with the harpooner Canonchet to the bow letting the lines down with spare harpoons by his side. The five other men sat under the sail, and Fralhem stayed at the steering oar, for two days straight, hanging on to the atlas and compass.

Sween kept to his Poe novel, with Witty looking down

on it behind him, Connell was whittling wood and Prestern was mouthing prayers.

Charlie kept on watch on every side of the tiny sloop, seeing more and more whales swimming, and breezing out of the surface on every side of them. They seemed to be getting closer and closer.

"It's like they're circling us," Charlie said but no one believed him.

The third day turned to the night. Charlie offered to take the oar.

"Fralhem? Shipmate? Would you like me to take the drive so that you can get yourself some rest?"

Fralhem gave an annoyed look, then shook his head no.

"I appreciate the offer, but I want to keep on course," said the third mate.

"We, we've noticed you haven't been sleeping so…"

Charlie began. Fralhem interrupted, "I said I'm fine! I'll sleep tomorrow."

Charlie curled down under the boat seat, next to the snoring Prestern, with a small stream of leaking water soaking his clothes, and foul smell of freshly caught fish that Canonchet had caught.

It was hard for Charlie to fall asleep in such an unconformable position; he rolled his shirt up in around pillow for his neck, yet after a long struggle he got tired enough to fall asleep.

"Bump." The longboat was moved as if it was a bath toy, making the sleeping crew jump up from their uncomfortable rest in panic and confusion.

After the hard hit it the boat rocked from side to side.

The men were all shocked and groaned in tired voices.

"Fralhem? What was that?" asked Canonchet, seeing the mate is nearly falling over the side, Prestern pulls Fralhem back in his seat as the lantern shook and swung like a broken lamp post.

Just when the mate was going to answer, the boat was hit again.

A sperm whale blew water from its blowhole sprinkling the frightened men as it gently pushed the boat on its lower port side keel with its huge head.

As the crew was soaked from the showering spout,

Canonchet grabbed a lance, in the hope of scaring the whale.

The native harpooner makes his way to the center of the boat, where the blowing water was shooting out.

Readying himself in position to stab it right in the hole, the man lined up his strike when all the sudden the spouting water stopped, and the whale stopped pushing and dived under the boat.

The strong rocking made the unbalanced harpooner fall head first off, the boat into the dark waters, just missing the massive wide tail.

The force from giant fluke made waves that pushed Canonchet far from the boat.

"Canny?! Canny?!" Fralhem yelled out holding up the glowing lantern as the only source of light, "Where are you?!"

"Herrrre!" responded Canonchet. "I'm far out here!" the man swam to the drifting boat.

Fralhem puts the steering oar back in the boat, Sween readied the remaining whale line, and tied a loop to the end.

Sween stood to toss it out when the boat was again attacked, another whale pushed the boat by its bow, making the man falls back breaking the wooden seat.

Seeing the line drop, Frahlem made Prestern take the steering, as he crawled to the line.

"Canny grab the rope!" yelled the mate, not able to see out in the dark, and only hoped Canonchet heard.

Canonchet swam on keeping his eye on the yellow glow from the lantern, hearing yells from the boat, then a tiny splash. After a few yards of swimming, he felt the rope with a loop on the end.

He pulled on the line, kicking in the water and climbed the rope is leading back to the boat.

"The line's tight sir," said Connell. "He must have it."

As Fralhem, and Witty tended unconscious Sween,

Charlie helped the Irish carpenter pull Canonchet back aboard.

The men heard whale howls and moans out all around them, it was clear they must have sailed right into the middle of a whale pod.

Canonchet made it back on the boat, but they were still in danger from the attacks.

The steering oar was taken right out of Prestern's hands, as another whale came along and grabbed the oar with its jaw.

"All stay seated and keep your arms in the boat," said Fralhem.

Throughout the entire night, the whales lightly pushed and shoved the boat around like it was a toy or a kicking ball, rocking it fore and aft, port, and starboard making the mast break down, and the sail blanketing over the crew.

The seven men bounced and fell on their backsides and head making their faces go green with sickness. When Witty was too scared to lean himself over the boat and could stand it no longer; then he threw up in the boat. The fish stench even worse with the stench of vomit.

Soon Connell, Charlie, and even Canonchet threw up from the reeking smell.

The entire night until morning the whales submerged under the water.

Leaving the single whaleboat drifting on the surface with the seven ill crewmen, sitting in the sea water holding on to their seats, some grabbed the oars while some curled up in his knees sobbing shivering both in fear and the cold of the wind.

CHAPTER 16

A Small Restraint

Later that day, Fralhem made spare oar for the new tiller, Witty tended the knocked out Sween, Connell patched up the cracks to stop the leaking, and Prestern, Canonchet and Charlie used a tin mug and can to scoop the vomit and fish guts overboard.

Just days after losing their ship the seven whalers suffering had grown worse. Their water barrel was still safe, and the remaining biscuits were dry.

Fralhem shared all the tack with the five men and saved the last big piece for Sween when he regained his conscious.

The day passed slowly, and with such low morale, the men said nothing to one another, Canonchet dropped down two fishing lines with bloodstained cloth in the water again, catching only small mackerels, Witty sewed the rest of the remaining tar rags into a second sail.

"Fear not my boys, fear not," said Fralhem. "Those dump brutes gave some push, but we still made it."

The men just gave him an enjoyable glance.

"They were playing with us," said Canonchet as the men looked at him with their ill faded green faces.

The silence wasn't broken until when late in the day Mr. Sween awoke.

"Ahh Wh!...Wh!...What happened?!" yelled the man.

"Good God! Are we sunk! Are we dead?!"

All the men looked at him wide-eyed as he made fast, aggressive movements, Sween put his hand to his head.

"Ow! Dear God, what the hell happened?!" he asked.

"It's okay keep calm man," said Witty, holding him by the shoulders. "You got yourself a nasty bump to the head."

Witty placed a wet rag to his scalp, making Sween yelp.

"Nice to have you with us," Fralhem said handing Sween the last biscuit. "You gave us a mere fright after we rescued Canny; you're lucky it was just a minor hit to the skull."

"Aye, you bookworms got stronger heads than hands," joked Connell, making some of the lads chuckles.

Sween got a few pats to his back; Charlie handed him his book, and then the man just laid down in the boat, slowly gnawing on the last ration.

The night came, and Fralhem still sat upon his stern seat, not falling asleep or showing any sign of exhaustion to his men.

The morning of the sixth day, Sween awoke to feel much better. Connell and Witty were whispering to one another, and the man comes close enough to listen to what they were saying.

"Tomorrow it will be a week since we lost sight of our vessel," said Connell. "And our Scandinavian mate looks as if we have much more to go."

"Yeah, I bet we will soon resort to the savage way," said Witty. "And he knows it; bet that's why he won't sleep or let any crew take the steering."

"I…I… think you both are overreacting," Sween said to break the meeting. "Fralhem wants us safe; we can't keep doubting him."

The two turned to each other, surprised how the college boy was now standing up for the third mate.

"Oh ho, the dandy bookworm now takes the Scandy's the word," insulted Connell.

"Shut up, and listen, your whining will not help any of

this, and just being the arrogant Mick, you are," Sween said when Connell's strong hands wrapped around his neck.

"What did you call me?!" yelled Connell, with Witty struggling to break it up.

"You know once the fish stop biting, and we go hungry, we'll have no choice but to turn cannibal."

Fralhem came from his seat to help separate the fight.

When he freed Sween from the choking, Connell pounded on him with his fist.

"You know it too! And it's in that Poe book of his!" Yelled the man, getting bunches back from Fralhem. "There is no land close by we're all dead."

Canonchet put down the fish he caught; to assist the fight. The Pequot grabbed the rope and tied it all around Connell with Fralhem's help.

After binding the man's hands and feet, they stuffed a cloth in his mouth, then lay him under the seats making Connell mumbles out swear words and shouts.

"Leave him tied up for a while; it'll do him some good," said Fralhem is looking at Witty shaking his head in agreement.

"And Connell, you try anything bad I'll throw you off." The mate smiled then made way to the steering oar.

Their sail only flapped, getting minor winds from the east, making the boat push slowly on through the strong choppy water.

Canonchet cut off two strips from the six fish he caught;

Sween got the first; he ate the second, Connell was fed by Witty putting it in his mouth, and when Fralhem got the last piece, he ripped it up to give the half to old man Prestern. "No thank you, sir," the old steward said making some of the men stare at him.

"You must eat," said Fralhem, holding it to the man.

"Mr. Fralhem, I'm fine, you eat it." Insisted Prestern.

"No, eat it now! Don't make this difficult," angrily stated Fralhem.

The steward hesitatingly took it, and despite being hungry, he slowly ate it.

"He must be thinking 'Why waste food on me?' Poor stubborn man." Witty whispered to Sween and Charlie.

CHAPTER 17

The First Storm

Gray clouds appeared ahead in the crew's view, as they slowly continued east. The cold wind gave the men chills as they shivered with fright, but Fralhem stood calm and kept the sail set. Coming closer and closer, the gray clouds turned darker and darker, and lightning bolts could be seen striking creating a white flashing glow.

"Mr. Fralhem? Are we to cut the sail lose?" said Canonchet.

"Wait, just a while when the wind gets strong cut it," answered the mate.

The men tied the equipment, tying the two lances and the last harpoon tight together secured the water barrel and the hammer, atlas, and sewing kit. Canonchet pulled in the fishing lines, and the nails were all placed in a bucket under the stern seat.

The sail was tightened from the strong growing breeze, making the boat move faster. Waves grew strong and splashed into the boat, soaking the men hanging tight to the boat's seats and railing.

The boat bounced on the waves, going under the dark rumbling thunderclouds.

When the showering rain began to pour on the sailor's shoulders, Fralhem took his knife and cut free the sail, making it flutter freely like a flag.

"Alright boys stay down, and hold tight," stated Fralhem as the boat was now moving by the pushing of the ocean.

The restrained Connell was laying helpless on the

bottom of the boat under the seat, rolling all around to his sides like a restless mummy, struggling to get out of his coffin.

He freed his fingers, pulled the rag out from his mouth and yelled.

"Oh, for Christ sakes! Cut me free!"

Before the carpenter yelled waves of water again poured into the boat, nearly covering his head.

"Oh God please! Get me out of here!" Connell screamed.

Charlie took Connell up by his collar, sitting him up.

"It's gonna be Okay," said Charlie, and before Connell could respond, another wave crashed in the boat.

Prestern, Witty, and Sween flung the pouring water over the side, out of the boat, using a can, hat, and cup.

Fralhem was directing the boat at a steady pace to prevent the boat from capsizing, as the waves turn bigger and bigger, changing from short, petty piles, into giant hills of water.

The boat soared down a large wave, like a long narrow sled, down in a hill. Canonchet sat in the front seat, holding onto the very fore side of the boat where the V shape was.

Seeing all of what lay ahead of the boat was absolutely nothing but stormy ocean.

Above in the sky where the black clouds and yellow flash of lighting.

"Ha, look, lads, the angels are bowling," Fralhem joked as he steered the sloop down the waves. Loud thunder shut out his voice from the men.

Charlie wanted to cut Connell free, but the boat was moving too fast. He was afraid he would accidentally stick him, so he struggled instead to loosen the rope knots.

Upon the oar mast, the rigging was violently swinging all around. Fralhem sat down off his seat like his men with his arms holding on to the tiller. Old man Prestern sat in the center where the mast was sticking out.

He stood and tried to lower the freely waving rig when a wave slapped the boat side. He held to the mast with his remaining strength to avoid falling over and cowered back under his seat in the flooding boat.

The men kept their heads out of the flooding water in the boat. Looking like a white wooden tub, they began to feel so helpless and shed tears like babies. None could hear each other above the roaring thunder above them.

Charlie hugged Connell and sobbed in terror. The Irishman's eyes turned misty, teeth grinding and arms gripping young Charlie.

Light from a thunderbolt flashed in the clouds for the crew to see they were coming to a mountain of the sea; there was nothing for Fralhem to do but give his boat into the waves.

The giant wave pushing the boat high up into the stormy sky made the whaleboat slide down the water mountain.

Fralhem sat up, noticing the storm had begun to die down.

His men were still sobbing bloody murder. His arm caught the tattered sail, and with his other arm he pulled it down, crashing it on the seat and shoulders of some of the men.

Though the boat was full of water, it still stayed afloat.

"Oh, my boys, wipe the rain from your eyes!" said Fralhem. "We made it!"

Rubbing their pained shoulders and shaking, they sat back up on the plank. They see over the stern of the boat that the clouds and the water began to die down. Waves became gentle, and the storm turned to a soft sprinkling rain.

"My God, he's right," Connell said to Charlie, still holding him like a loved one. "We're still floating."

CHAPTER 18

The Second Storm

It had to be morning since the dark gray became lighter and the men believed they'd made through the whole storm. It was now day seven since the separation from the ship. The men now poured the water out of the boat, luckier that all the supplies made it, and the fresh water was still clean from salt.

The only thing that was lost was Sween's book.

"Oh damn, my only pleasure that can soothe me is now lost," said Sween after digging through all his pockets.

"You must like to read," said Canonchet. "Have any other books?"

"Yeah I had five books, said Sween, "I left, back aboard the Mako."

"Christ, you brought your own library," said Connell pouring a bucket full of seawater overboard.

"Yep, I had Mary Shelley's Frankenstein, Shakespeare's Macbeth, Hamlet and Melville's greatest novel ever Moby Dick. Now I've lost Pym's narrative," said Charlie apologetic.

"No worries, I have dozens of Poe's poems back home," Sween replied. "If we ever make it home."

"Are we to put the sail back up, Sir?" asked Prestern.

"No leave it down, it's not over," said Fralhem seeing the light gray turn, black again.

"Oh no!" said Witty in a panicked voice. The other men had faces of fear, worry, and discomfort, and thought unpleasant thoughts.

The wind kicked up again, and waves pushed the boat

on every side. The men now prepared themselves and sat below off the seat planks.

Fralhem brought in the steering to let the boat drift along the tide.

Rain poured hard on the crew's back soaking them, making the color dye in their clothes fade pale.

Thunder roared like a giant lion and flashes of yellow bolts shot down, from the clouds. The only difference in the second storm was that the waves were not so heavy and only light splashes got aboard not so much flooding like the first storm.

The boat lightly rocked fore and aft, making Connell, Witty and Sween sick again, as their face turned green and threw up this time over the side.

Fralhem still kept the water barrel and tools safely under his seat. He kept his compass and Sween's atlas book tucked into his shirt.

Despite it getting soaked, Fralhem had to keep the atlas safe since it was the only source of chart aid they had.

It was turning darker and darker. Too wet to light the lantern, so the men held on to the boat blind in the pitch-black darkness.

"It's alright boys, no matter what happens, do not let go of the boat," Fralhem said.

"Aye sir!" replied the six men holding to the single mast, the boat's railing sides, and the plank seats.

In their seated positions, they feel water coming up, as more and more waves splash over the side into the boat.

The water grew over their knees, then covered their whole legs and began to rise to their waist.

"It's alright men, keep her steady," said Fralhem sitting back on the stern. Splashes slapped up in his face, making him cough out the salty liquid.

The boat was again filled like a long oval shaped pool, heavy and nearly under the surface, but despite the weight, it stayed afloat.

A foot of seawater now covered the inside of the whaleboat, but the waves were still light, so Charlie thought it was smart to take up the bucket and empty out the water.

Standing up in the boat's puddle with the wooden pail, keeping a balance with a plank between his legs, Charlie scooped water out the starboard side.

"Whatever you're doing up there, stop it and sit back down! "ordered Fralhem unable to see Charlie standing up in the middle of the dangerous squall.

Hardly hearing what the mate said, Charlie, took up one bucket full when a powerful bolt shot down from the sky striking right to the boat's side, creating large ripples that hit the boat making it capsize.

Charlie hit the water first with the wooden bucket.

He held on to the wooden bowl as his only lifebuoy and it made him float away from the capsized boat.

The five sailors swam from underneath, climbing up to the boat's keel while underneath, Fralhem held to a cleat. He felt the atlas fall from his shirt as his arms waved around, blindly trying to catch it.

Far worse he felt a hit to his knee as the fresh water barrel fell from the boat sinking down to the deep.

Forgetting the atlas, Fralhem tried to catch the water supply, but it was already gone.

"NO!" yelled Frlahem's underwater voice, as he swam up for air.

He breached to the surface with a strong grasp for breath, then made to the turned-up vessel.

"It's alright boys, hold on!" said Connell. He, along with Witty and Prestern held on to the port side, while Canonchet, Sween, and Fralhem held to the starboard.

"Oh no! Evekins, he's gone," said Prestern.

CHAPTER 19

Fished Out of Danger

All men that night shouted and screamed for Charlie Evekins, now lost in the storm. Throughout the rest of the evening, up to the following morning, the rain finally died down, and it was time for them to fix the swamped boat.

The Irishmen, and two blacks Prestern and Witty, joined Fralhem, Sween, and Canonchet on their side, to help flop the boat back over.

It was easily done, but the entire boat was full of water and the snapped mast was still attached in the center.

Fralhem made Sween get aboard first to drain out the boat.

The shortest one in the crew climbed in and gave his five shipmates' oars as buoys to hold on, and a rope to keep them from drifting away.

Sween grabbed the cup and tin can and started to haul out all the water.

Emptying out the boat's hull for almost an hour, it was half cleared, and the rest of the men climbed aboard.

By the eighth morning, the boat was emptied of seawater.

After suffering through the second storm the tired and hungry men laid down to rest in the wooden haul.

Fralhem who'd had the least rest of the group was grunting and cursing out loud in his Norwegian tongue, making his crew worried and concerned. Some wanted to ask what was ailing him, yet no one bothered to say anything.

Many thought it had to be the loss of Evekins.

In Fralhem's mind though was the loss of the water and

atlas. The water supply was all gone, and he and his men may not last another couple of days, even thinking they might not last another storm.

"What now sir?" asked Prestern.

The mate looked to the steward, then he shrugged.

"You all should sit back and rest awhile," Fralhem answered. "And in time we'll have to just row out from these waters."

Far off in the middle of the teal blue waters, floated Charlie Evekins holding onto the wooden bucket as his only source of floatation.

The entire night of holding on through minor waves and stinging rain, the lad had made it through but had no idea where his boat was.

Frightened, tired, and confused not knowing what to do or where to go.

All he could think was just to hang on to the bucket with the remaining strength he had left.

Below his legs began to get numb, so he started kicking his legs around like a Cossack dancer, making him move backward and hold the bucket to his stomach like an otter.

Then his heel felt like he kicked a rock, making him shout in pain.

Looking down in the water in panic, he feared it be a shark.

He stopped with the motion of his legs and curled them up touching his elbows.

Turning his head down in the sea, he was not able to see anything but his white shirt.

His heart pounded against the inner ribs of his chest, he breathed heavily, and tears flooded the sockets of his eyes.

In the mind of the young sailor, Charlie Evekins, he

thought it was the end, to be either devoured by sharks or lost forever, drowned far deep into the ocean floor.

He saw a dorsal fin sticking up from the surface then a second and a third, all swimming in different directions, and beginning to circle him.

Evekins didn't panic, just shed a minor tear, and accepted the coming fate. All he hoped was it to be done quick and painless.

A shark began to swim close up behind him and the sailor gripped the bucket tighter than a farewell embrace, and tightly shut his eyes.

Grinding his teeth, his eyes hard shut, he waits to be attacked, and killed in the jaws of a shark, but nothing happened.

He didn't peek or loosen his grip; he still took hold and kept his legs from moving.

When his patience grew shallow, he opened an eye to see no dorsal fins.

He opened both eyes and looked in all directions to find nothing but the teal water and gray pillows. He kept his legs curled up, feeling they were still just lurking under him, waiting for a limb to dangle. Then right from under it came.

It was the young bull who breached to the surface, right near the lost whaler.

Charlie watched the entire form of the whale submerging then go back under, first seeing its dark side eye, long left fin, wrinkled hump ridges, and finally the wide triangular tail.

The fluke flopped right into the air above him, and before it could slap, Charlie dived down, to swim a distance from the mass.

Underwater, waves pushed Charlie around like a fluttering leaf with one hand gripping the pail.

He opened his eyes in the stinging water and saw that

it was the young orphaned calf, with the long hemp whale line dragging behind it and tangled around its dorsal ridge. Charlie went with his free hand and grabbed on to the rope, and made to the surface, coughing and splashing with a bucket and rope.

From yards ahead was the young whale, and the line attached to his jaw, grew tight as it began to pull the whaler from behind.

Charlie held to the long rope, dragged along the surface like a fishing bobber. Ahead the whale submerged again, creating waves, making the castaway up and down, like a surfer.

Times when he got pulled under and backed up from the bucket he hooked his arm around the line with his hand gripping on the line.

CHAPTER 20

Hauled Again

Aboard the long whaleboat, Fralhem put his tired, starving crew to the oars, to row out from the stormy sea.

The men performed sloppy rowing, with grunts, moans, and the oars tapped and banded together, making sounds like fighting bucks.

The lazy crewmen slowly pulled the oars and kept their eyes down on the puddle of seawater below, that was tiding fore and aft down the vessel.

Fralhem, at the steering oar, stared at Sween's spare compass, the last navigation aid, still keeping the boat heading west.

Sitting hunched down on the seats, with legs tight down, and hands gripped to the oars; the crew continued to row weakly like children, making the boat move real slow.

"So where are we going too, sir?" Prestern asked.

A few seconds past and Fralhem turned his head to answer, and before he could speak a whale spout caught his vision in the corner of his eye.

The mate placed the compass in his pocket, and then stood up looking at the shooting water.

With a clear view, he saw it coming.

"It's a whale!" pointed Fralhem. The crew halted the oars and turned to see.

The young 40-foot bull whale was half above the surface showing his dark gray hide, small dorsal hump and splashing tail.

The whale swam out about 60 feet away from the

whaleboat, then dove down with its fluke making one last splash and was gone.

It must be the orphaned whale," Canonchet said, with the rest of the boatmen looking at the mate. Fralhem said nothing. When he turned to his men to order them back to the oars, a voice came to his ears.

He looked around to see where it came from.

When one of the men was gonna, say something Fralhem shouted, "Quiet!"

The voice was like a strained whisper from the wind, and it came back, but this time he knew what it was.

"Here!" a voice shouted from the sea.

"Do you hear that?" the mate asked. The men looked to all sides; Prestern, from the center, stood and then Canonchet stood from the bow seat to get a better view.

"Over here!"

"Where is that coming from?" asked Witty.

"Perhaps we're losing our minds," said Sween. "Just hearing things…voices."

"Men! I said quiet and listen," said Fralhem. "There is someone…"

Before the mate finished the whale came up from the portside, breaching out from the surface and comes jumping out from the teal water up into the air.

The giant round head soared over the boat; its side fins were spread out like tiny wings of a bare featherless chicken.

The sailors kept their heads up, staring at the whale's smooth light gray stomach as its entire mass jumped up and over the boat.

Their heads then turned to the starboard side, as the whale crashes back into the water. Sinking down like a fallen boulder, soaking all the boat crew, and knocking the three standing men back down on their seats.

"Lord above, ever seen a whale do something like that?"

Sween said to Fralhem who didn't answer him all stayed silent.

The mate was bug-eyed with amazement and stiff as a dead corpse.

To the bow side sat Connell, who turned to ask the harpooner the same thing.

"What of you? Ever saw one jump over ya?" asked the Carpenter.

Canonchet turned to Connell and slowly shook his head, then lightly replied, "Never."

All the crew just sat with amazed expressions on their faces, especially Mr. Fralhem.

In his head, Fralhem was now starting to think that his men were right and that the very whale they had made an orphan was the one who pulled them far away from the ship. It stranded them out in the ocean and more to this that it had now followed them.

"Hey! Out here!" the voice came back to his hearing. "There it is again!" Fralhem shouted getting back up on his feet.

Looking to the port where the whale had emerged and looked at the small blue waves, he spotted something. A speck of white and brown bobbed on the surface.

He pointed his finger right out at it. "Look there men, tell me you see it?" ordered Fralhem. All the whalers stood from the plank seats to look out to the port side.

"Oh, my Lord," stated Prestern, "It's Charlie."

Smiles grew across all the men faces and cheering laughter screeched out from the boat.

No words were said as the men put back the oars and Fralhem turned the boat to the drifting Charlie.

Holding to the wooden bucket and the loose hemp rope,

Charlie's thoughts were all happiness for being rescued from the dangers of the shark-infested waters.

The boat was approaching the castaway and the mate could see Charlie kicking his way to them.

"No, stay where you are! We'll come to you!" Fralhem yelled out.

Canonchet turned from his seat to ready a rope. He looked up and saw Charlie swimming his way when he saw a sharp dorsal coming straight up behind him.

The Pequot dropped the line and yelled out,

"Stop swimming! There's a shark!"

Hearing that, Fralhem yelled again to Charlie to stop kicking his legs and stay still.

In the water, Charlie turned his head, and he saw the Grayish brown fin sticking up out of the water. Then it's head came up fast revealing the rows of sharp teeth from its jaws.

Before the man could even curl up his legs, the shark was already upon him and he felt sharp teeth penetrate his leg.

A scream of pain shouted from Charlie, and the men stopped with the oars to see him atop of the water. It was Charlie stuck out from the surface, with a large stream of blood waves behind him and a tiger shark's tail swirling all over in the water.

When the moment came with the shark passing under the middle of the boat's port and with no hesitation Prestern stood up and leaped right onto the shark's body just behind its dorsal fin.

He nearly turned the shark over on its side and made the shocked fish loosen its grip.

Charlie kicked the shark's nose with force and made for the boat.

As Fralhem kept his eyes on Charlie, Prestern treading

on the surface behind him, the crew could see more sharks appear on every side of the boat, like crocodile killing a lone injured hippo.

"Oh, Christ boy get in!" yelled Connell. "Sharks everywhere!"

Prestern came to the boat, as Witty and Sween's arms stuck out ready to grab him. Canonchet could see a coming Tiger shark swimming toward the old man's legs.

He stood from the seat with his last harpoon tied to the line.

The Tiger shark approached the starboard bow less than three feet away.

When the dorsal past, he tossed the iron from his hand, piercing between gills and the second fin.

The shark violently wagged its tail, along with the harpoon. Sween and Witty got Prestern aboard, and the shark missed his legs.

The shark weakly swam to the boat's, stern slowly pulling out the line.

"Mr. Fralhem?!" yelled Canonchet. He tossed the mate a lance.

Fralhem took the spear and stabbed the shark in the head. A second strike to the gills making the shark stop moving.

"It's dead, we got it," said Fralhem.

The men looked down on the large shark, and within seconds smaller sharks came all around. Blues, Makos, and White tips swam up to nip pieces of flesh from the dying tiger shark's carcass.

"What are we doing?" said Canonchet. "We should haul this fish aboard!"

Fralhem looked away to his harpooner.

"Aye, you're right, that's a load of meat right there."

The mate hooked his lance in the shark's nose, and Canonchet pulled the hemp line.

"Alright you slugs, take the fins and pull it in!" Fralhem ordered.

The four men looked to the mate.

"You want us to bring this…" Connell tried to ask but was interrupted.

"I said grab the fins!" Fralhem yelled.

More sharks kept ripping flesh off, and the four men took the frontal and top dorsal, pulling the 12-foot striped shark aboard the whaleboat.

The shark had at least ten bite marks on its port side, and the left fin was bitten off, but more shocking to the men it was still alive.

The men took out their pocket knives, and Witty grabbed his razor. Canonchet took out his harpoon, then Fralhem readied his lance.

"Let's kill it," stated Fralhem.

The tired, weak Charlie watched from the end seat of the boat as his shipmates stabbed the Tiger shark to death.

Late to the coming sunset, with the smell of rare meat and blood flooding in the puddle water, Charlie watched the men cut the shark up into meat strips.

Fralhem and Connell cut off the head and bottom jaw, reaching down its esophagus, pouring out more and more blood. Small dead fish that floated belly up in the boat's red puddled water.

Prestern, Sween, and Witty removed all the remaining fins and tail. Canonchet cut opened the abdomen, taking out its heart, liver, long yellow stomach filled with small decayed fish, squid, and kidneys.

It was harder for him to finish because of the little light, but the shark was mostly empty of blood, organs, and what was last eaten.

"I think this will last us a week, don't you?" asked Sween holding a meat strip to his face.

"Let's hope so," said Prestern in a full mouth voice, chewing on his shark meat.

Fralhem cut a piece of the shark's heart and was going to give it to Charlie, but when he lit the lantern, he discovered,

Charlie had passed out.

Fralhem let him sleep and ate the piece himself.

"Don't get too crazy men; we should save this bitch to get us through a few days," said Fralhem, leaning on his lance like a walking stick.

All the men stayed awake, not able to sleep because of the foul stench. Some took off small pieces of flesh from the shark's gutted body and placed it in their mouths as a midnight snack.

CHAPTER 21

The drifting Nightmare

The days went by, and it was now day 18 the 9th May 1860, Fralhem believed they were far off course in getting to Tonga, because of the two storms had blown them southward in between the Tonga Isles and New Zealand, somewhere above the Kermadec Trench.

Fralhem decided to set the boat south and make for New Zealand's north island, as the shark meat would help them from starving.

Canonchet, Sween, and Witty sat next to the dead Shark carcass, and Connell and Prestern took the other side and went back to rowing. After a morning the crew began feeding on the shark's organs, the heart, and kidneys, they had their strength back.

The storming sky turned white gray and the thunder sounds disappeared, more sharks came up circling the boat.

Charlie Evekins was still passed out. Fralhem laid him beneath his seat and placed his gray-bluish jacket under his neck to keep him comfortable and dry from the blood puddle in the boat.

As Fralhem directed the boat south, with his right hand on the tiller, and his left holding Evekin's boney fingers.

Charlie made small, catlike moans and sighs, and twisted his head slowly side to side as his grip on the mate's hand grew tighter. Fralhem thought he had a dream.

The dream began with all darkness when Charlie's eyes slowly blinked open and he was on the boat.

The whaleboat was full of blood and bones, but worse they were human bones.

Looking at the ocean which was the color of organ and yellow, like flames, black dorsal fins began to stick out from the surface and circle around the vessel.

From above, the bright sky was the same color as the sea, only more of a dark yellow with ugly black clouds. Flashing purple lightning from the crack of the pillows swarms of gulls came flying all around like vultures that had spotted road kill.

Charlie discovered that his physical form had changed. He was more overweight, and bloodstains covered his clothes, and he had utensils in his hands.

He screamed in horror as he realized he had eaten his shipmates and was in hell.

He screeched like a panicked woman and then heard repeated shouts "Wake up!"

Charlie awoke to Fralhem and Prestern holding his arms.

"Well Heaven's above, we thought you'd never awake," said Prestern. "You've been screaming for hours."

"You alright? Charlie?" asked Connell, looking over Prestern's shoulders.

Charlie was hesitant, then quiet, and slowly replied, "A nightmare, it was just a nightmare."

"Well from what you went through I'd have bad dreams myself," said Fralhem.

He reached behind and grabbed a piece of raw shark.

"Here you should really eat something." Charlie took the meat and slowly devoured it.

"Well we're glad you're alright, we'd almost lost you forever," said Prestern patting his back.

"Aye, happy to have you back Charlie," said Fralhem. "I was sad and lost with every hope when you were gone."

"So, did I," quietly replied Charlie.

The morning of the second week, the gray storm clouds began to float farther and farther away down the horizon, and the bright colors of the dawn began to crack out from the east; it was to be a bright, sweltering day.

The seven whalers sat in the boat with the shark carcass.

They had already stuffed their stomach with raw organs and continued to pick off flesh from the decaying shark.

Canonchet and Fralhem began to cut off and save some body pieces, such as the eyes, dead digested fish from the cut opened stomach and strips of the intestine to use as fish bait.

And though Fralhem ordered the men to slow down with eating the shark meat, they still ripped off strips with their bare fingers, making the shark look as if it was a fish that was tattered by eagle talons.

The boat crew were all silent, with bored misery in their eyes and mind.

Men said nothing to one another and just stared at the dead shark.

Fralhem was still at the tiller, looking ahead of the boat.

The mate too had a miserable exasperation in his eyes.

The 14th day was clear blue skies with the burning sun drying and stinking up the dead carcass, yet the whalers had no aspiration of sickness as if they grew used to the stench, no longer feeling sick, becoming more tan from the beating spring sun.

CHAPTER 22

BACKSTORIES

In the middle of the day, the men ripped off a hand full of dry shark meat.

Charlie was eating a part of the dorsal fin; he looks around to his shipmates.

"So, you had yourself a bad dream?" asked Witty, when Charlie's eyes caught his.

Before Charlie could say yes and tell him what it was about.

Connell interrupted. "Well share it another time, cause I'm in no mood of hearing unpleasant things."

All men looked at the Irishman and nodded their heads in agreement.

"Where are you from?" asked Charlie.

"What? Why?" Connell asked.

"Like you said, let's not talk of unpleasant things, we should speak of good things, like home and loved ones," said Charlie. "So where are you from, Mr. Connell?"

The Irish carpenter looked to the other men waiting for his answer.

"Cobh," Connell answered. "I came from Cobh and left because of the "Gorta Mor" in 49, just me and me only surviving family, two wee lil' sisters."

"What are their names?" Canonchet asked.

"Debra and Denies," Connell answered. "They're both twins with cherry red hair and hazel eyes. More important, they're safe back in New Bedford, with their well-off husbands."

Hearing a story of home and family gave the men slight joy giving them the reason to live and make it back home.

"You're lucky to have a remaining family," said Charlie, patting Connell's shoulder.

Witty was eager to share a story, and he spoke next, after Connell stopped talking.

Here is Sam Witty's story:

"I came from a planter's farm near New Orleans and ran away from the plantation fields with my momma and brothers when I was ten years old, by stowing away on a riverboat that took us north up all the way to Chicago.

I started sailing in the Great Lakes, till I decided to go to sea.

We moved to Boston back in '55, and I decided to jump aboard whaling ships, and strike an oil fortune, never once had a slight worry or dreamed of being lost out in the big ocean."

Tom Prestern's story:

"Well, worry not brother Sam, we'll get out of this, and you'll see you, family, again," said old Prestern.

All the shipmates smiled at the old man and listened to his story.

"A long time, in fact, my whole youth, I worked as a house servant in the big houses of Newport, until I fell for my wife who was a house maiden.

We quit the miserable unfair house slave jobs and went to make something of our lives, and we did. We had ourselves a daughter. My lady was a stay-at-home momma, and I started as a barrel maker, earning to put food on the table in our small home at Fair Falls. When my wife passed away, my little girl, Andrea was only 12."

Now I'm a single parent, and I worked more long hours until I made enough to put her through school. As she grew into a lady like her momma, she became a tutor for our people who couldn't read. And when she turned 19 she met herself an excellent strapping barber.

They fell in love, married and a year later I became a grandpa.

So afterward I wanted to make more money to leave for my grandchildren by joining a whaler and like aboard all ships they make the old black fart the cook."

"Well, you do a good job in it," said Witty jokingly. "You make a good supper fit for a king."

"And your daughter and her family are the reason why you must make it back," said Sween, with Prestern nodding.

"Let's hear it, sweet Sween," said the Steward.

Owen Sween's tale:

"My life was in schools, books and indoors. Cut away from the real world; my whole family was into two trades, law and education. I have an uncle who is a professor in Philadelphia, an elder brother, sister and three aunts who are school teachers. My father's side was law.

So you can say, I done well in school, well enough, and I got myself a scholarship to Havard and Boston. My father wanted me to be a lawyer like he was. Before I started, I learned to speak fluent French, Spanish, Italian and Latin. Father thought I could become a good diplomat, but I still wanted to go my own way.

"Yet first chance I got, I signed up to the Nantucket whale fishery, though it was against my parent's wishes. I wanted I go out around the world before I entered a career because I'm still struggling to find what I really want to do in life. I started as a child in school doing office work, but I came aboard to work in a life of physical, manual labor in the harsh, endless, brutality and power of nature. Out here in the ocean, thousands, and thousands of miles from home. I still don't think I want this to be my permanent career in life."

"You still have a lot to go through and much ahead," said Canonchet." You'll find something."

Matthew Canonchet shared.

"I was born to a fishermen father and net-making mother in Groton. I was the first of four siblings and started sailing out with my dad, fishing at the age of six.

I got interested in whaling when Pa's boat beached on Watch Hill, where we discovered a dead right whale washed ashore, and we spent the day cutting the meat off to share it with our neighbors. Most of whom were struggling on the reservation of Connecticut, who had no luck inland hunting and had a failed harvest.

When I turned 13 back in the year 1843, I went to New Bedford and signed aboard as a common decker; nothing else was expected of me except just washing the deck, and knot tying.

It was just three months out, off the coast of Caicos Island I struck my first whale. The white harpooner was clumsy and was too scared to give the whale the harpoon. The officer was angered and had me take the strike, and I did.

We came close to the giant, and with a signal hit I tossed the iron right into the whale's eye; a signal harpoon killed a 70-foot bull whale, and from then on, they made me the harpooner. After the voyage of two years, we returned to port with 1600 oil barrels. With the money I made I used it to support my people on the Algonquian reservations.

Upon the return home of my first voyage, I met my wife Aleshanee, a Nauset beauty from the cape, and we made six children together."

"Wow, six kids?" asked Sween.

"Well, we had seven," corrected Canonchet. "Our latest was stillborn. Yet it still stays in our hearts, and I really wish to get back to them all."

Throughout the day, the crew shared some of their personal stories of life ashore and loved ones, the pure reasons that made it worth living and surviving this voyage.

All through the heart-to-heart tales, third mate, Fralhem stayed silent, even when his men looked to him if he would like to say something.

"What of you sir? asked Prestern. "Got any family?"

The mate just nodded, with his eyes closed. "A little brother maybe."

"Well, how is he?" asked Canonchet.

In Fralhems mind, he didn't want to talk about that, yet he felt it would be unfair since his men had shared stories of family. Yet he only answered.

"I only know he is back home in Norway; he's 20 years old now, and I left him," said Fralhem.

"Why did you leave him?" asked Connell. "Did you blame him for your mum's death?"

Fralhem nodded. "I blamed no one. I left to pursue my dreams; I wanted to go to sea and be a ship's captain. I left my brother safe in the care of orphan keepers and besides, he's grown up and left the orphanage by now."

"Do you ever write or even think of going back for him?" asked Sween.

"Well I did leave him a small note with some money that was left for us when he turned 18," replied Fralhem. "He legal age by now so he's long out of there."

"Do you miss him?" Sween asked.

Fralhem took off his cap and put his head down.

"Can we talk of something else?" he asked.

CHAPTER 23

The Bleeding Erik

"How about the Erik of Torunburg? right?" asked Witty.

Fralhem's tale of the Eriksson.

"The Eriksson of Tonsberg," Fralhem corrected. "Well, it was back in the year 1852, in the Norwegian Sea, north of Faroe and East of Iceland.

The single hull beneath the deck where we ate and slept was loaded with barrels full of Mink blubber and baleen, yet still, need to be filled before returning.

"So on a fall season dawn, we were following a lone bull sperm whale migrating southward. It was quite large, twice the size of the Eriksson yet we wanted to take the gamble.

I was at the head rowing seat, with the harpooner behind me.

The single sail was set, and we rowed to make it faster.

We caught up to it. We rowed straight from behind and brought in all the oars. I watched as the harpooner, struck the beast in its black body.

He managed to get two harpoons on it.

The whale must have been twice as long as the boat, yet we weren't afraid. We thought it be just like our previous kills and that this would be no different, but we were soon wrong.

"The beast didn't swim out panic or frightened, like it should've, it just swam under.

The lines from the harpoons dragged out off the railing.

Yards were pulled out by the hundred, so the captain had us tie one to a cleat and the second around the single mast.

That turned out to become a stupid plan.

"We watched stupidly as the line ran out and instead of pulling ahead at the bow, the whale turned to our left and dragged the Eriksson by the whole side.

Soon the water poured over the side and just when we knew it would, the longboat flopped.

I was holding on to an oar hook, and under the cold unmerciful dark blue sea with the light of the morning sun shining through the surface, I saw the mast brake right off like a twig, and the cleat snapped right loose.

I swam in the air pocket right under the boat that used to be the deck.

I went for the hatch, to see if I could gather things like food or fresh water barrels, but when I opened it, gallons of blood and meat strips from the minke whales we had slaughtered spilled all over, blinding my sight from black to red.

I gave up that idea, swam under and upon the surface.

Swimming past the dragon head to the bow, I climbed up on the keel and saw most of the crew had made their way up on the red hull of the capsized vessel.

There were now 15 of us all together, but the harpooner was missing. Last, we saw he was a hold and dragged by the mast, being pulled from the whale far out for miles.

"We yelled for him to let the mast go and come back, but he never returned. For we knew he was lost, drowned or have frozen to death.

Now all of us were stranded on an upside-down, 40-foot-long ship and cold, wet and helpless. We were in the middle of a cold sea in autumn.

"To help raise the body temperature up, we held each other by hugging, wrapping our limbs around each other like a couple making love and endured the foul breaths to our faces.

I had to do it with an old shipmate of mine, Lars Korkens, an old man from Christiania, the ship's blacksmith.

Together on the keel, we laid back on it, like a wooden beach with our breaths stinking up our noses and warming our faces.

"A cold day passed and night came. The cold water, steam, and ice drifted around us. The air, freezing us all over, was the least of the danger.

The first night they came, the orcas, the wolves of the sea.

Many of the crew sat up and pointed to the long black fins.

The killers circled us, more aggressive than sharks, banging against the boat's railing, knocking off some men down into the water, but they manage to climb back on and held onto the boat's keel.

It was clear that the orcas sensed the whale meat and the blood that spilled out from the hatch of the deck and now they were after us.

They were hunting us like penguins on a drifting iceberg. Soon it got worse than just hitting the boat as one orca jumped to the stern side, pushing the other side of the boat up and knocking three men in the water.

"I managed to hold tight to the boat and saw a sailor being dragged away into the water with a blackfin behind him; half his body was in the jaws of the black, and white killer, he was screaming and screeching like a slaughtered pig.

Another man was pulled right down, like a turtle head.

The captain, of whom I can't remember his whole name, but we did call him Leif, after the real man who found the new world was armed with a boarding spear.

He flipped it around and handed the wooden handle end to the last sailor in the water and pulled him back on.

Yet our captain got injured cause he was holding the

blade end of the spear. He badly cut open his hand, and we had nothing for bandages.

That first night we lost three men and our commander was wounded; none of us slept that night.

“The second day the killer whales were poking the deck below us as though they were feeding on the whale flesh from the hull that we butchered, and we can hear them chew, and moan like desperate, starving beasts.

“That day we counted all the whales; there had to be a total of 20, swimming in all directions around us.

We had nothing to defend ourselves with, except the boarding knife.

We were cold, hungry, thirsty and scared, like helpless cowards. We had nothing to do but sit on the top of the capsized ship.

“I noticed Captain Leif’s hand became all red and had nothing to stop the bleeding. I decided to remove my scarf and give it to him as a bandage. He thanked me, then handed the long boarding knife to me.

And I remembered the order he gave: “Kill any orca that come near you,” he said as he wrapped the scarf around his hand.

The second night came, the orcas struck again. A large male jump from the boat bow side where I was sitting and with its large body mast, pushed half the boat down below the cold water, soaking my pants.

When the orca wiggled off the hull, it floated back up, but my shipmate, Lars lost his grip on the cleat.

I reached my hand out to him, and he caught it. His feet were dangling in the water, as another sailor was trying to pull him up.

“It’s coming!’ yelled one of the men.

A killer whale swam up and took old Lars by the leg.

I had another man take him by the hand, and I was going to strike it.

With a three-foot blade of a six-foot boarding spear,

I stabbed it by the nose, making it scream and spout a chimney of fire, squirting blood all over our faces.

It made it bite down harder, and Lars' right leg was ripped right off.

"We pulled him back up to the keel and tried to tend to his wounds, but through that night he bled to death real slow and painfully. The following morning, there was a stream of his blood spilled down the hill of the hull.

I wanted to keep his body up on the boat with us that night, but the men removed his coat and shirt.

The next morning his body was frozen solid, and we decided to let him go.

Lars' body rolled off the hull into the ocean and a young killer whale dragged his body down.

"When the fourth day came, three men had frozen to death and now only half the crew was left of the Eriksson.

It was that night I slew my first whale.

The sun of that fourth day began to set, and that was when an Orca attacked.

It breached the surface, and its mass landed right to the hull's side, again trying to push it down.

I nearly lost the boarding knife, but it was caught by Captain Leif, who tossed it to me.

I stood up on my knees and stabbed the black killer right in the head, pushed it deep down, so far, I must have pierced it directly through the melon, int its brain.

It screamed like a panicked lady giving birth.

It violently waved its head around, pushing the boat up and down, knocking some men off the boat into the water.

The boarding handle almost decapitated me, as it swung right by my face.

The killer whale moved aside, right back into the water, soaking us with red sea water violently waving its tail and fins.

Soon the orca died from its wounds and turned belly up, exposing its giant white belly.

“That was the very first whale I’d killed. I watched the killer whale pack push the dead body away from the Eriksson, and they never returned.

That night we lost two more men to the cold and I believed I too was going to die, having no food or water for days and the cold began reaching all over my body.

“Finally, on the fifth day, a merchant ship found us.

A Scottish fur trader ‘The Margaret Maiden’ from Leith, rescued us, eight survivors.

We were all weak and close to death; we were practically down with hyperthermia. And they had us wrapped in blankets and thick brown bear hides they traded from out of Archangels Russia. They fed us hot chowder and warm tea.

“My blood began to warm up again, and I could finally feel my finger and limbs again, but now my toes. With all the strength I’d gathered, I unwrapped myself removed my boots.

When I removed my thick, damp wool socks. Two toes of my left foot were pitch black from frostbite and my big toe on my right foot. Though I was disappointed, yet happy it was just small parts of me and not a whole foot or leg.

When I showed my black toes to the Scottish captain, he promised to have a doctor see to them when we made it to port. And he gave me dry, warm socks.

“While making a functional recovery, the Margaret

sailed north leaving the Eriksson behind to sink. Two days later we made it to Iceland.

I went below to tell my mates from the Eriksson the excellent news, but the happiness was not to last as that evening, we Norse whalers discovered our Captain Leif, had passed away from the cold. The Scots tending him told us he was down with pneumonia, died just when we made to land, and our suffering misery was at an end.

Afterward, when the Margaret docked in Reykjavik, we survivors stayed awhile in a boarding house and sent a report to the Tonsberg Whaling company. We waited for a vessel to take us back to Norway.

When a message came from the Tonsberg ship owners a week later, they sent their regards to the lost whalers, but no payment for what we all had to go through. They practically sacked us and asked us not to bother returning to Tonsberg.

"We seven survivors from the Eriksson all went our separate ways, many went back to Scandinavia, but I decided to go to America.

I managed to get a passage to take me west, and the ship brought me to New Bedford. There I lived in the boarding homes, coffin houses and train stations working my way around to earn pocket money and paid my way in a school where I learned to read and write English.

"After my short schooling year, I decided to restart my life back to the sea, in the Nantucket Whaling fishery and that was where I met my new shipmates, Branter and Tisburn and have been sailing with them ever since.

Fralhem ended the story.

"That's one hell of a sea story," said Sween. Mr. Fralhem didn't respond but just stared out at the open ocean, watching the transitions of the sky colors as the dusk began to darken the sunset scenery as if the lights were slowly burning out.

CHAPTER 24

HUGGING THE CHEEK

Days had now become weeks of being lost at sea, and it was now the 28th of May.

All the men learned to the boat side with their head between their shoulders looking down at the water.

Behind the men, in the bottom of the boat was the skeleton remains of the Tiger shark; its skull, a pile of teeth, and dozens of spinal columns remained. They have depleted the fish, and every piece of its flesh was eaten leaving only the bones and a puddle of blood soaking in their trousers.

Canonchet tried to catch fish but on all the hooks he pulled up, the bait was missing; no fish were biting, but tiny reef Minnows were nibbling off the bait.

The hungry men also suffered from thirst; they try to restrain from drinking the sea water and the smelly salty, sour red blood from the shark.

Fralhem, who still sat on his stern seat by the tiller, had no rest nor sleep. He would angrily yell at the men not to drink it, for it was mixed with salt water and would increase their thirst.

Fralhem too was getting weak in the sight of his men.

Bags began to grow under his eyes and the tone of his voice was thick and deeper, like an angry old man down with a sore throat.

For them, luck had run out. For they now felt sorrowful for eating the shark and began to cry.

Yet they didn't wish to show it, and that's the reason why they kept their heads looking out to the sea.

Charlie thought of how lonely he was on land and yet was now just as miserable out to sea, even though he had friends with him. The hunger reminded him of his time out on the street having no friends, food, or anything that made life worth living, until he joined the Mako. He was now stranded on a boat, thinking of the time he was a homeless boy from Salem perhaps was less bad than his present situation.

He then thought of the dream he had, of him eating his shipmates, soon the thoughts turned suicidal. Charlie felt that he should die first for his shipmates since they have families and homes. They have better reasons to return home, he thought he should die, and his shipmates could feed on his remains and have a chance to make it.

But knowing Fralhem will deny him to do it, Charlie just knelt down with his hand cupping his face.

In his swelling eyes trying to dry out tears, Witty was twitching and blinking, looking in every direction in front of him from blue sea to hot sunny sky.

He saw a dorsal fin of a shark came out and Witty dragged his arms back in, but still watched it swim around the boat.

The sounds came to their ears; the cries of the gulls.

Gulls by the hundred came flying around like bees circling their hive.

The other men began to look to the birds and Charlie thought it was an omen from the nightmare.

Yet for Fralhem it was a good sign.

"Bird! Wheezed Frlahem "Bird… could mean land's near."

Some of the men could hear the quiet dry voice and the gull screeching was getting louder and louder.

Witty sat up then turned his head to the sea again and

saw something that sparked all happiness and erases of unpleasant thought.

Witty had found it.

"Land!" he shouted, the crazy hair tailor pointed to the boat's starboard side. Every man turned to look.

Far away just peeking from the horizon was a dark green patch in the shape of a mountain.

"It is... It is!" shouted Connell. "Land!"

The men shouted and laughed.

"Oars to the water!" ordered Fralhem.

The men who heard spread the order and with weak rowing, they made for the island.

As they were rowing nothing was said, for they were too happy and eager to get on dirt and soil again for the first time in nearly a year.

Slow moving with hours of weakened rowing and with loud heavy breathing, the boat crashed into the sandy beach, and the starving whalers pulled the oars in.

The Pequot harpooner on the bow seat was the first to touch the sand.

His bare feet sunk down in the wet sand, he walked up holding a line attached to the boat. He walked and walked until the sand felt dry.

He dropped the rope and fell on his knees holding handfuls of sand.

Soon the other men came rushing onto the beach. Men who had shoes on ripped them off to let their feet feel the land.

From behind the happy crowd was Fralhem.

Splashing through the waves with wet sand dirtying his boots and trousers, he crawled up to the dry sand. He took in armloads of dirt as if he was hugging it. Then the Norwegian officer fell face down in the sand.

CHAPTER 25

God's Tear of Land

The sailors stopped embracing the sand and made their way to the jungle line.

The men stood in a line, sniffing the smell of the island and dry land: there was no more salt, blood, fish, or human vomit. Finally, smelling jungle, tropical humidity, and island flowers.

Canonchet led the party in the jungle, leaving the mate behind on the beach.

Through the jungle, with the sun shining through the canopy, the forest floor was dirt, small rocks, twigs and dead leaves. The men put their shoes back on as they explored the thick of the land.

The sailors cared not if there would be a town or habitation to come across, the men were too mindless and carefree as they wondered through jungle seeing new colors of green and brown and no more colors of blue and gray clouds.

Hard, loud chirps and caws came from the birds.

Little rodents and lizards speedily scattered around to hide in their small burrows.

The whalers made their way through only two blocks of jungle when they found water.

In an open patch of the jungle was a large pond.

"Water," Canonchet said aloud.

His white and black shipmates ran past him. They dropped to their hands and knees and dunked their heads in the pond, drinking the clean water, as did the harpooner, drinking the water like animals.

Charlie submerged he was drying out his watery eyes. He saw someone in the jungle, peeking through the trees.

But when he blinked to get a better look, there was no one there.

He looked to his side and counted the men and that one was missing.

"Fralhem!" he yelled to himself.

The men watched as Charlie ran back for the mate.

He saw Fralhem still laying down in the sand next to the boat.

"Fralhem? Fralhem?!" Charlie yelled coming to his side, and turning him on his back.

The mate's chest and face were covered with sand.

Charlie brushed some of it off and tried to wake him up.

"Come Fralhem you must wake," Charlie said. Fralhem only responded with grunts and moans.

Charlie took him by the arms and dragged him to the jungle to get him to the pond.

After dragging the past out officer for a while, Charlie stopped for a breather. He laid the man back against a tree trunk so he could catch his breath.

While standing in the jungle, stretching his limbs and taking deep breaths, he saw it again, a person looking directly at him.

And he was able to make it out as a woman.

"What the?" he asked aloud. He turned to Fralhem who was still passed out on the tree stump. He looked back, but the woman was gone.

"Maybe I'm going mad," Charlie said to himself, "I need to calm myself; been at sea too long."

Again, he dragged the mate to the pond and placed his face in the water.

"Come on Fralhem," Charlie said.

The mate quickly got out of the water coughing.

"You're trying to drown me, just when we found land!" he said jokingly, coughing out water.

When the officer was wide awake, he took his fill of fresh water and went with his crew to hike up a large grass hill.

On top, they got a full view of where they were; it was a small island with two ponds, with an open grassy hill and has wildlife.

Prestern and Witty gathered firewood, and with his dry matches they made a good roaring flame, keeping them warm as night began to follow.

"Well boys, I'm not entirely sure, but this could be one of the Kermadec Islands. Clearly, it's deserted," said Fralhem, putting his hands near the fire. "But no chart or the atlas, I can't be so certain. Hopefully, we're near New Zealand. This seems a good island; we'll hold up here for a while and hope a ship will pass."

As the men sat around the fire, Charlie wanted to ask his friends if they had seen a woman, yet he decided not to, and dropped his strange sightings.

Before the men went to sleep on the island grass, both Connell and Prestern held hands with the rest of the crew to say a prayer.

"We all thank ye Lord, and Christ in high Heaven above, for looking to us and coming in our hour of need." started Prestern. "Great Father, Son, and the Holy Ghost thank you for giving us this small tear of land as a chance for our salvation, we are and will always be grateful to you," Connell ended.

Then all the men said in a clear voice. "Amen."

CHAPTER 26

Temporary Marooning

For the first day, on the island, they let Fralhem sleep by the died-out fire pit as the men searched the whole island.

Canonchet and Prestern wanted to catch something to eat.

Connell and Witty went back to the boat to gather the tools, and bucket for drinking water.

Sween and Evekins were to search around the beach areas to hunt for crabs.

Connell, got his hammer and nails, along with rope and the tarpaulin to use for shelter.

Witty got his sewing kit, mirror and gathered some of the shark teeth.

They returned to the spot-on top of the grassy hill and found Fralhem curled up in a ball making noises.

"You alright, sir?" asked Witty when they approached.

The mate lifted his head.

"Oh, I didn't know you guys would be back," stated Fralhem wiping his eyes. "Huh… Nei! Nei! No! No! I'm fine, I just awakened and was just yawning."

"Are you feeling alright?" asked Connell Fralhem nodded and replied. "Just hungry. I know Canonchet will find food."

Witty and Connell left the materials from the boat with Fralhem to organize them and began building a shelter while Witty and Connell gathered twigs for another fire.

Connell made it up to the hill first and on his face was a shocked stare.

"You alright? Mr. Connell?" asked Fralhem.

The Irishman then dropped all the wood, Witty came from behind and did the same thing.

Fralhem turned and looked out to the view of the ocean.

Far to the horizon was a moving brown mast with sails.

"It's a ship," said Fralhem quietly. "It's a ship!"

Yelling out loud, soon Witty and Connell yelled the same thing.

Prestern and Canonchet were walking from the jungle with two dead Swamphen birds. They saw Witty and Fralhem waving their arms out and shouting out.

They ran up to the top and saw Connell had made a fire.

"Canny! Canny!" yelled Fralhem. "There's a ship!"

The men dropped the game and looked out and could see the ship far off.

A half-hour past, Connell, and Canonchet made smoke signals with the tarp. While Fralhem and Prestern were shouting, Witty, went to look for the other two.

As they shouted and screamed, the men noticed blood spilling out from the mate's mouth, yet they stayed focused on the passing vessel.

Prestern turned around and saw Witty, Sween, and Evekins coming up.

The whole crew was now shouting and waving as the fire blazed stronger and stronger, yet the ship showed no sign if it had seen them or not.

"Good Christ! What's keeping them?" asked Connell.

"She's too far off, and they'll bypass us."

"To the boat!" said Fralhem spitting blood.

Fralhem made Prestern stay up the hill, to man the signal fire, as the rest ran to the boat.

Rushing through the jungle, tripping on some branches

and mud, they made for the beach, only to discover the boat was missing.

"What? Please tell me were on the wrong side," said Connell.

"No, there's the boat!" pointed Witty.

They looked out and saw the whaleboat drifting out by the tide, away from the island.

Sween and Canonchet rushed to swim for it, but shark fins appeared, and they retreated.

Connell, dropped in the sand, yelling, and cursing, same with Sween, and Witty.

Fralhem patted Canonchet, and they both nodded.

"We're marooned," Connell said in a sad tone.

"We'll have to keep the smoke up; maybe they'll stop here for a resupply," said Canonchet.

"Don't lose hope now, we'll make it," said Charlie, helping Sween, and Witty up.

"What the hell? How could this happen?" asked Connell as they made their way back to the jungle.

"It was just bad luck and carelessness," answered Canonchet.

Back to the meadow hill with the fire still roaring and Prestern was trying to wave out more smoke to the ship that was still sailing out of sight and behind him came the crew.

They informed him the boat was lost and they are now marooned.

After a small silent and a fade of hope, the ship disappeared. The men turned to the mate and found out what was ailing of him.

"Fralhem, sir what bothering you?" asked Charlie.

"Nothing," he answered plainly.

"Don't say that," said Canonchet. "You're coughing blood and constantly moaning in pain, tell us!"

"Are your sick sir?" asked Prestern.

Fralhem nodded an annoyance as he wiped the blood off his chin and neck. "It's not a sickness; I just lost a tooth," he answered.

"Is it scurvy?" asked Sween.

"I don't think so, just a rotten tooth," Fralhem replied.

"It's nothing of concern, and there's no need to worry about me, honest."

"Well if you're in pain again let us know, so we can help," said Canonchet.

Fralhem just nodded and waved his hand, as he made for the pond to wash his shirt.

CHAPTER 27

The Previous castaways

Three days later, the ship passed the island after a total month of being lost. The whalers made their shelter on the north-west side of the island where the ship by-passed, and every day one man was stationed up on the hill to look out for another vessel with Prestern's dry matches.

They only used Canonchet's striker set to make the beach fire.

The crew filled their stomach on birds, rats, crabs, fish, and mussels.

They used the big pond with cleaner water as their source of drink, while the smaller pond was used to wash their clothes and sometimes bathe in.

Canonchet who had left his harpoon and lance back on the boat made a spear crafted with shark teeth as the blade.

Connell was the one making shelters and a tiny raft Canonchet could use to fish on off the beach.

Witty, Connell, Prestern and Sween were put busy with other manners, such as gathering firewood, scouting the beaches and jungle and foraged for bird eggs.

Charlie was up on the hilltop on his watch, sitting next to the ash pile in the fire pit.

The view was from a clear meadow hill next to a clear water pond, surrounded by a dark green jungle top, and then far out he could see vast, teal-colored ocean and the light cloudless sky, with clean white clouds.

It looked like a painting from the Renaissance.

For Charlie, it was like the first time he saw a ship when

he drifted his way to the New Bedford port city, and he sat along the beach near a lighthouse, watching dozens of vessels pass in and out from the docks.

Charlie pictured it as heaven and even wished he had a pad and set of paints to keep the scenery. He sat up for hours staring at the pretty view, with a hat he had made from jungle leaves that used shade his head and neck from the hot sun.

"Hey Charlie?" yelled Connell. "Day's up, and it's my watch now. So did you see anything out there?" he asked Charlie.

"Well no ships, but a beautiful view," Charlie said pointing out.

"Hmm, yes it's quite a scene, I saw something like it back on the green hill of the Cork coast," Connell said, looking at the pretty scenery.

"Have you seen anyone else around?" asked Charlie.

"What are talking about?" asked Connell.

"What I'm saying, have seen another person on this island, like a woman or something?" Charlie asked.

"I ain't seen no woman," said Connell, with a smile growing on his face. "Did it look like a naked cannibal trying to eat ya?"

"After a few chuckles, he patted Charlie's shoulder, he knew Connell didn't take him seriously about the woman he'd seen, even when he asked the other men, they say they had seen no one and that he had just been at sea too long.

So, Charlie left his Irish shipmate on the hill spot and decided to walk around the beach.

It was late in the day near sunset, and he was walking to the Western side of the island, where he and Sween had been crab hunting.

The western side was mixed with sand and pebble rocks

and a 10-foot high rock cliff with jungle vegetation hanging off it. He knelt down to gather rocks to throw in the water when he discovered something strange on the rock beach. It was two rock piles.

The piles were neatly stacked and placed neatly like they were covering something and on a closer look, he realized the two long piles were the size of humans.

"They're burials," said Charlie. "People were here."

The two rock graves were covered with seaweed and tiny crabs. He dropped his pebbles and made for the beach camp to tell his shipmates.

The next morning, Charlie led all the crew to the two graves he found.

"Those are bodies under the rocks," said Canonchet.

The men gathered around the sight; they discovered two sticks there were pushed to the ground by the tide, and they were tied together in the shape of a cross.

"They were Christians," said Prestern.

"And French," said Sween.

"How do you know?" Asked Witty.

Sween came from the rock cliff and held up an old green glass bottle.

"There's a melted word on this bottle that, Du Vin.

That's French for wine," translated Sween.

"And look what else I found."

He walked then to the rock cliff, and Sween pushed the old leaf hanging off the rock, and revealed scrap writing on the stone.

They were the names and date of death of the two bodies in the rock piles.

"Jacques 1856 et Letizia LaCapet 1857."

Then there was a small carved phrase, writing underneath that read,

Avec Les Angels."

"Yeah see?" said Sween "It's French and it reads "With the angels."

"My God, dead for years," said Witty. "You think they starved?"

"I don't know," said Sween poking his finger to his head,

"but by the looks of it, they were stranded here, and must have been here for quite a long while, or the other theory I have is that a ship past here and decided to bury the couple on land.

Just a guess but it's possible…"

Then Charlie spoke up.

"No, the girl must have buried them."

"What girl?" Fralhem asked, rubbing his cheeks.

"Oh, that woman you keep sighting around?" Connell asked, still not believing him.

"Yes, she must have been stranded with the LaCapets, and her time alone has made her afraid, so she's hiding from us," answered Charlie.

"Oh please," stated Connell. "Stranded on an island for years, and new people come on it, who might help her off, and she's afraid? Rubbish."

"Aye, he's right unless she's too dumb, or way too shy," agreed Witty. "There can't be any girl."

"Only because you men haven't seen her," said Charlie.

"Well, in any case, we should continue in trying to get off this island," said Fralhem.

"In what way?" asked Sween. "Maybe these people waited for a ship and none came."

"Well, we'll wait just a while then, we'll plan something," said Canonchet.

The men made their way back to the camp on the beach

when suddenly from off the rock cliff was the sound of cracking branches and a scream.

The men turned and saw it was a young girl, who had fallen from a tree onto the beach.

"Good God we're not alone after all," said Connell.

The girl got up unhurt shaking in fear as all the men stared at her.

The girl was young with pure raven hair, red tanned skin, wearing a brown two pieced, ragged dress.

"Hello, are you hurt," Charlie asked.

The girl just violently waved her hand, shook her head and shouted words they couldn't understand and then she fled into the jungle.

"Well, she's definitely either shy or crazy," stated Witty.

"Jesus. What bothers her?" asked Fralhem.

"Well either someone else buried these people, and that girl is not so intelligent to do so, and was just abandoned, she's probably a feral child, more of an animal to understand humans."

"We should help her," said Charlie.

"Well, she didn't want your help," said Canonchet. "And she's too afraid that she ran off like a frightened squeal and maybe Sween's right, that there's no helping her."

"Yeah, if we make a way off this island, we'll try something to aid her," said Fralhem. "But in the meantime, let's not waste any of our time."

CHAPTER 28

Concerns and Preparations

A week after discovering the late islanders and the mysterious savage girl, the castaways began working on a raft with Connell putting together lashings, with branches and hemp line, with the help from Witty, Sween, and Prestern.

The raft was built with two long jungle trees to even the balance when floating. Then they tied strong branch lashings together to make it into a long rectangle like a drua. The idea came from Fralhem, yet the men were not comfortable about going out to sea on a raft and wished they had the whaleboat.

"I don't like it," said Connell. "I mean a raft is an obvious choice to make in getting off an island, but honestly I don't trust it, as a carpenter, I prefer using bigger trees for a reliable raft and using a stronger line since we're running out of rope."

"Well, we'll make rope," said Fralhem cooking crabs, on a fire.

"Well, I don't think that will hold very long," said Connell. "And especi..."

"Look, no need to argue about it!" Fralhem interrupted.

"At least we'll have something to get us off this cesspool, so just build it."

Fralhem took a crab leg, cracked it open and took some meat out.

He placed the meat in his mouth and as he began to chew, he let out a loud, painful yelp.

"Ow!" he screamed, spitting out the crab.

The men all dropped what they were doing and went over to their officer who was rubbing the sides of his head, with his mouth wide open.

"Oh, Lord! Sir, you alright?" asked Prestern.

He took his hand, and placed one of his behind his neck, then the old steward took his head back to look into his mouth.

"No. No, it's fine," said Fralhem. "It was just a piece of shell."

The mate lightly pushed them away and covered his mouth and plainly said, "Thank you."

The mate went down to the tide and took some sea water to wash out his mouth.

The men were standing at the jungle line when Canonchet and Charlie returned from hunting.

"It must be bad," said Sween. "Whether it's a tooth or gums it hurts him when he eats. He can't go on like that; it's bad enough for him not sleeping, but if he has pain when he eats he won't make it."

Despite many worries from his men Fralhem still refuses to let his men look in his mouth.

Other than a toothache, and sleepless nights, the men noticed Fralhem was miserable on the island as if he wanted off more than any of them. He'd help collect more lashing for the raft and ordered Witty to make another sail from the tarp.

The leader of the lost whalers shuts himself in his own angry mind, from the misery of his molar.

Even when sitting down to eat around the fire, they watched him keep his head between his knees, not eating his share of fish, or bird like he was punishing himself for every mistake and mishap his men had.

The men were scared for him, yet they don't know what to do; even when they suggested removing his lousy tooth, would help, but they didn't have the heart to do it by force.

The raft was finished within ten days and made in the shape of a rectangle and over 16 feet long. Despite being completed, the crew that put it together refused to use it.

So, the men talked their mate into using the raft, only when a ship is spotted.

CHAPTER 29

COLLECTIONS

Sween returned to the camp with two French wine bottles.

"Where did you get that?" Witty asked.

"Found them by the graves, of course," answered Sween. "We can use them."

He placed the bottles by the pit, to use for fresh water from the pond. The next day, Sween and Witty returned with a wooden crate and found four more bottles.

"Christ! Where these people marooned with a winery?" asked Connell.

"Maybe, but we're finding more stuff by those two burials," answered Witty.

"Well, I wish they left us full bottles because I could go for a quick one," Connell joked.

"Aye, I miss a drink myself," Witty said sitting next to him.

"So, you're finding a crate and glass bottles?" Fralhem asked Sween.

"Yes, we're finding some other stuff around that side of the island," said Sween. "It must have been their camp before they passed away and could be useful."

So, the next day Fralhem send Charlie and Connell to help find more stuff they could use.

Again, they found empty Du Vins bottles, an old ripped up net, another wooden box, dozens of empty, rusted vegetable cans, and some old Bilge hoops from barrels.

So, with a total of 18 empty Du Vin bottles, they filled them up with pond and rainwater, used the crates as a cage to keep caught crabs and smelt the old can together to make it into a wide frying pan.

Other than collecting crabs and fish they caught from the water.

Canonchet and Prestern would climb the trees to steal the eggs from the birds they hunted and raid swamp hen nests in the meadows and use Connell's hammer to break and dig through dirt and rock to catch rats and moles.

So the men began rationing all they could catch to be ready when another ship was spotted, and if they can't catch a ship they might as well continue out to the sea, yet the men still were scared of using the raft.

Late on the 20th evening on the island, the men all sat down around the fire pit, to a full dinner of roasted pelican and crabs.

Prestern said a small prayer thanking the Lord and the hunter Canonchet for catching the big bird.

Connell proposed a toast.

"Well, here's to us the lost whalers of the Mako, may our story live, whether we all make or not."

All men raised their shell cups of water.

"Here! Here!" all the men said.

After raising their drinks, they brought them to their mouths and began sipping water from the hole of cleaned out conch shell cups.

"Hey!" shouted Witty spitting water from his mouth.

The men turned and with the light of the fire they could see the girl, peeking from the side of a tree at the jungle line.

"Well, I'll be," said Prestern. "Look who decided to come over for supper."

"She's not coming over," said Sween. "She's like a dog and she's going to wait for all of us to sleep, and then she'll rob us of our food."

Connell was about to stand.

"No! stay seated," ordered Canonchet. "Let's wait; she's observing us to see if it's safe for her to come closer."

So all the men turned their eyes to the young girl, who was still staring at them. She stood there like a shocked deer, who'd heard a hunter, yet she still didn't run away.

Minutes became hours, and no one made a move.

"Oh come, men, can't you understand?" asked Charlie.

"She's probably hungry."

He stood up and put a slab of bird meat on the forged plate.

"You're wasting your time; she's going to run off again," said Fralhem.

Charlie strolled around the group.

"Hell," he said to the girl. "Are you hungry? We have food and we'll share."

Coming a bit closer, the girl made a slight jump as if she was ready to flee, but she didn't.

Charlie halted, placed the tray of meat on the ground, then the conch of water beside it.

"And we have fresh water." Charlie turned back to his group.

He made them all sit in a circle around the fire with most of their backs to the island girl.

"What's she doing?" asked Connell, about to turn.

"No, don't turn around, just keep eating and look to the fire don't turn to her," said Charlie.

After a while of staring at the flames, he asked Canonchet, who could still see her.

"Is she taking the meal?"

Canonchet smiled and nodded yes.

He saw the girl kneel down, sat crisscrossed on the sand and begin to eat.

All the whalers ate the pelican, made small turns to the girl, who still stayed a distance away from them.

When she had finished her meal, she then stood up and held out the clean tray.

Charlie came up with Sween behind him. As they approached they saw she was sweating and shaking like a stage-frightened actress, but she didn't run off.

Before Charlie was about to grab the tin tray, she said her first words to them, in very poor English.

"I…uh good…tas… it great," she said in a cracking pain voice.

Charlie was amazed. "She can talk," he said to Sween.

"Well, very poorly. Either she forgot to talk, or her English is very limited," replied Sween. "But Perhaps she remembers her native language."

CHAPTER 30

The Island Girl

Charlie had Sween translate for them and have her come closer, to sit by the fire.

When Sween repeated his request to come to join them in French, she replied. Then Sween repeated to Charlie,

"She asked are you the crew's leader?"

Charlie called for Fralhem.

"Oh, looks like you're gonna meet a girl, sir," said Witty.

"Alright Witty, go to the hilltop. Then morning will be your watch, now get lost," Fralhem said and walked off.

Prestern and Connell went to their shelters to get some sleep.

Fralhem walked over. Charlie came and wrapped his arm around the mate.

"Now tell her this is Mr. Fralhem, our ship officer," said Charlie. "And that we're castaways."

Sween repeated all in fluent French.

Then she answered back, clear and calm.

"She says her name is Alasia, she's 18 and pleased to meet you," replied Sween. "Also thanks us for the meat, says it tasted good."

"Let's have a seat by the warm fire and get better acquainted," said Fralhem. "Then stand here in the cold dark."

The night passed as Charlie and Fralhem learned the island girl's story as it was translated by Sween.

Alasia Maleia LaCapet was a native of the French

Polynesian Island of Papeete and her parents were merchant traders who came from the city of Marseille.

They moved from France, into the overseas trading business in the French provinces off the coast of Africa and Indochina.

Alasia was their only child and was born after her family purchased an estate on Papeete. She grew up in her youth exploring and traveling from island to island, all over the Pacific, from far as Japan to Tasmania, from the Galapagos Islands to Formosa.

She and her parents came to the island when they had to jump the vessel, due to the severe damage it sustained from a hurricane after leaving from New Guinea.

On a lifeboat with six crewmen from the trade ship, they drifted for ten days until they came across the island.

They had over four crates of imported wines aboard the boat. When they beached on the land, the crewmen were so overjoyed they broke into the crates drinking bottle after bottle, getting themselves drunk.

Her father Jacques tried to govern the men, yet they were too ignorant, worse foolish to command.

It was only the next morning. One sailor attacked his wife. He tried fighting off the man, but his shipmates helped beat him down, so bad that they killed him.

The sailors then went for Alasia and her mother, but they hid in the jungle for days avoiding the sailors. After just two days, the six sailors gave up and decided to abandon the women on the deserted island. They took the lifeboat leaving the two women with nothing but empty wine bottles and Alasia's deceased father.

Then a year later her mother died, leaving her alone for the last three years.

Alasia's stopped saying more, she then stood up and said a few words to Sween.

"She said that's her story and she says she'll be going now," translated Sween.

"But wait," said Charlie. "Can you ask her if she wants to bunk here?"

Before Sween could say anything, she was already walking to the jungle.

"Looks like we need to earn more of her trust," said Fralhem. "But I'm sure she'll be back."

Fralhem was correct cause the next morning when all the whalers awoke to make a breakfast of bird eggs, Alasia returned. She had brought along a sizeable fancy-looking trunk case.

Charlie went over to assist in carrying it closer to the group which she at first refused, but she had been lugging it through the jungle all morning, so she allowed him to help.

"Is that her own treasure chest?" Connell joked.

Sween then asked her in French what was in the box.

She didn't answer and just looked at all the men, took out the key around her neck, then unlocked it.

"Probably a bunch of lady dresses, and perfumes." Witty joked to Connell, who nodded and laughed.

Fralhem got up and walked to where Charlie was, and they looked in the opened chest.

"Good Lord, it's navigation equipment," said Charlie.

Fralhem and Charlie knelt, for a closer look.

"There are three compasses, charts, a sextant; everything we need to find our way home."

Fralhem was grateful for the girl's gift and ordered Connell builds her a shelter next to theirs.

"Well, I want you boys to forage for more supplies for our departure. We will be leaving in one more week."

CHAPTER 31

JAW PAIN

A chip of a rocky cliff, Fralhem ordered Canonchet, Charlie, and Prestern to gather more game and fresh water from the jungle.

He had Connell and Witty work on a mast and sailed for the raft and Sween stayed with Alasia up on watch on the hill and tended the shelter on the beaches.

During the time spent on watch, Sween taught Alasia English.

In the hunting group Canonchet and Charlie notice Prestern was coughing and wheezing heavily.

They reported it to Fralhem but when he asked old Prestern, the old Steward would tell them it's nothing of concern.

By the morning of the 26th day on the island when all were around the fire to eat.

Fralhem walked up with Prestern.

"Well boys, Mr. Fralhem needs your help," Prestern said. Every man looked at the mate and saw his mouth was puffed up as if his cheeks were swollen. "He needs to have that rotten molar out, and he requires your assistance."

All the men and Alasia walked to the headland part of the island, a 50 foot drop off near the LaCapet graves.

The men noticed Fralhem was shaking in fear as if he was going to be hanged. Prestern patted his back and then discussed their plane for the removal of the rotten tooth.

"Now boys we have no pillars or doorknobs. But Fralhem thought of a way of getting out the molar. Connell, Sween,

Charlie, and brother Witty take him by the arms and hold him tight. Mr. Fralhem felt the tooth and said it's weak and coming loose. So, it's now, or there will be more pain."

Fralhem slowly knelt on his knees, shaking and sobbing scared. The four oarsmen held him by the arms.

Prestern opened the mate's mouth and pulled out the cloth that was stuffed in his cheeks which made Fralhem a moan of pain.

The Steward puts up his head, with his mouth wide open and tied a long string around the rotten molar, the first one on the top left jaw.

Canonchet on the other end of the line tied it to an old heavy two-foot long log.

"Gosh, I hope this works," said Canonchet.

Fralhem nodded in agreement with more tears coming from his eye sockets. Charlie could feel his heart pounding hard like something was gonna break out from his torso.

"It'll be alright, sir," said Charlie. "We're here for you."

"Alright, I'll count to three, and Mr. Canonchet will drop the log down the cliff" stated Prestern.

Alasia came from behind the officer and tilted his head high up, and his mouth was opened wide.

"Ready?" Prestern asked Canonchet.

The harpooner nodded, as he headed to the end of the cliff.

"Right, 1…2…" The men all counted, with Fralhem huffing heavily, staring into Alasia's eyes, as she patted and rubbed his head.

"Three!"

Canonchet dropped the log down the cliff and a tight tug, the molar came straight out of Fralhem, making the mate scream in agony. The men kept a strong grip on his arms, Canonchet and Prestern looked down watching the log fall straight down until it hit bottom.

Fralhem kicked his legs around like a mule, but the crew still kept hold to his arms. He screamed for a total of nearly five minutes till he loss conscious, slowly passing out, seeing Alasia's eyes before he fell into a coma.

The night came, and Fralhem never woke.

"You think we should leave on the raft?" Witty asked Canonchet.

"No, I still don't trust it," said Connell. "It's not strong to carry all of us to New Zealand, we need a boat."

Canonchet and Prestern agreed, they must stay, and wait for a passing ship.

CHAPTER 32

Fralhem's Dream

Opening his eyes, he could feel no hard land below him, but cool thin air in every part of his body.

"What is this? he asked himself. "I can't feel anything."

He tried standing up, it was all dark, and though he could not feel anything, he could hear the wind, waves, seagulls and moans not moans of a human but loud, eerie moans like a giant, old, lame cat.

He turned in all directions as he walked blindly, not knowing where he's heading until he can hear his feet kicking water.

He just kept walking, with anxieties filling his head, wondering where he was and where his men were.

"Charlie! Canny! Prestern!" he Yelled aloud but hearing no echo, just sounded as if he were yelling in a small empty closet room.

Still hearing more of the queer noises humming all around him.

Confused Fralhem put his hand to his head, covering his face.

To his surprise, as he brought his hand to his mouth, and poked his finger to where his rotten tooth was, he still felt it.

"What the? I got my molar back?" he asked himself, then placing both hands to his head, completely covering his face, he said in a worried, panicked voice, "Oh Lord, what's happening? Am I dead and in Hell? What is all this?"

He took his hands off his face and saw a light.

The light was a horizontal line the color of blood orange far away.

"The sun? The horizon?" he wondered. The light raised higher and higher lighting the scenery, or the ocean, clouds, and the beach he was standing on.

In a blink of the eyes, he saw a boat. An empty boat just drifting to the beach.

"Why can't I feel the waves against my legs? he asked. "What is going on?"

The loud groans and strange clicking noises became louder and louder, when to a surprise, a spout of water shot out from behind the boat, pushing the boat right up in front of him.

The boat washed into the sand and the water drained down, exposing the whale behind it.

The creature was beached on the land, unable to get itself back to the sea.

Dumfounded, not knowing what any of this means,

Fralhem was about to walk aboard the boat when a figure moved past him. The character was dark, and Fralhem couldn't identify him; it was in the figure of a man, who was armed with a long spear.

The figure came to the whale, which was flapping its fluke, and fluttering it fins, helplessly trying to get away from the man with the spear.

The man stumped his boot on the whale's side and slowly drive the weapon down into its lungs. The last things Fralhem heard was the screams of an infant then the scene he was staring at went black.

"What the?" he said.

The screams of the baby silenced, then a different set of noises came to his ears.

The sounds were of thunder bombing like cannons, and loud splashes like waves.

The final set of sounds were voices. They were the voices of humans but not of any languages the mate could understand, but they were loud cries, screams, shouts and sodding hopelessness, as if it was coming from full grown men who never learned to talk from childhood or had lost their speech. Fralhem believed the sounds had to come from men.

The sounds of the storm went away, but the sobbing of the adults continued.

Fralhem didn't bother to say anything, thinking it utterly pointless, yet his mind was filled with total confusion.

Out into the real world back on the island.

The whalers brought their mate to the beach where they laid him down in his shelter with Charlie and Alasia looking after the unconscious officer.

Fralhem lay on the sand, twisting and turning his head making minor grunts from the mouth with the small piece of cloth that was put in by Prestern.

"My, I hope he'll be alright," stated Alasia, rubbing the back of his scalp and tightening her hold on his hand.

"Me too," said Charlie, staring at the mate's discomfort.

"Can't believe the courage of this man. Must have taken a lot to agree to go through so much pain."

"Yes," nodded Alasia. "More courage, guts, and bravery than any knight of an adventurer; he'll make it."

"He must," said Charlie. "None of us will make it without him. He's gone through much and will go through more to get us home."

The night came, and Charlie and Alasia never left Fralhem side. And throughout the evening the two talked endlessly of their past lives.

Returning to Fralhem's strange dream.

Sitting blind, hearing the sounds of crying men, light finally came into Fralhem's view.

Light shone and revealed a new scene. Fralhem was sitting in the stern seat of a whaleboat.

The boat was leaking of red like blood, with dead belly up fish, and empty floating wine bottles.

With a blink of his eyes, he saw the source of the crying sounds. It was four dark figures. All were sitting in the boat curled up with their arms wrapped around their knees and Fralhem could hear them all cry like they had given up.

All around the boat was open ocean and clear skies from a boiling sun.

The boat was moving as if it was dragging something real slow and was unbalanced, as it was about to capsize or sink.

The mast in the center held a loose rigging, with a tattered cloth for a sail wrapped around it that just fluttered freely in the weak wind.

Fralhem stared for a long while at the men in the boat.

When he heard seagulls screech in the sky, he looked all around and to a surprise he spotted a ship.

"A ship? Hey, there's a ship!" Fralhem yelled to the men pointing out. But the crying men made no move and said nothing.

Fralhem stood from his seat and walked to the bow.

When he passed through the mast and ducked under the rigging and before he was going to step over one of the dark crying men, something hit him.

It was a hit so hard and painful it made him trip off the boat into the sea.

Fralhem treaded to the surface and tried to get back to

the boat, but the boat drifted away, and he began to sink under the waves.

The more he tried swimming, the more he sank down like he was in quicksand. But when he tried to stop struggling, he sank down into the sea completely sinking like a lead ball.

As he kept going down and down into the depths looking at the hull of the boat getting dark and smaller, he could also see small heads poking out from all sides of the boat.

He waved his arms trying to swim up but to no avail, and just kept sinking and in the end, his sight went black and he began to gulp water.

CHAPTER 33

FALLEN TO A LIKEN

"Hold his arms," said Alasia, with a hand on Fralhem's forehead and another to the bottom of his chin.

Charlie restrained the mate, and Alasia waited till it was safe to put a finger in. When Fralhem stopped chomping at his jaw, and the cloth was in her view, she stuck a finger inside and got it out of his mouth.

"Right, got it," she said.

"You make a good nurse," said Charlie. "And your English is getting better and better by the day."

"Father wanted to put me in schools back in France, but mother was like my personal tutor. She even taught me some English, since they did business with them."

That evening the two sat by the flame near Fralhem and talked through the night endlessly.

Alasia discussed the traveling she'd done along with her parents, about things they did together. Goods they traded, captains, nobles and native island chiefs they met and how they spent little time at their estate back on Papeete. It was just her and her parents with the whole world as their real home.

Charlie shared the story of his homeless life on the streets, of going into the whaling business, and his time aboard the Mako.

"So, you hunt whales?" asked Alasia.

"Well, not really," answered Charlie. "Just a common sailor. The harpooner and mate are the ones that slay the whales."

"What's it like aboard a whaler?" she asked.

"Hard living and cruel," Charlie said. "I love the ships and life as a sailor, but the whaling life… Like if I knew how gory and dangerous it was or I would end up being lost at sea, I just would've been a simple fisherman and slept back on the streets as a tramp."

"I see," she said. "Well, you made it this far. You seem quite the survivor of just a simple homeless man."

"So are you," Charlie replied. "Yet you survived on this island alone without your parents. I wouldn't have made it without…this man," He looked at Fralhem who was moaning and grunting as he slept.

"Well I guess we have something in common," Alasia said taking the hard-tough hands of the two sailors. Charlie wanted to say more, but he watched her as she eyed the poor officer lying in a coma on the sand with a coat for his pillow, just lying down in peace breathing through his nose.

CHAPTER 34

AWAKE

Two days passed. Fralhem was still unconscious, and Charlie never left his side and nor did Alasia.

Most of the boat crew was gathering more fresh water but the past few days, dark rain clouds came over the island and rain began falling which gave the stranded whalers more water to catch from the jungle leaves.

All but one was up on the watch hill.

While Charlie, Alasia, Prestern, Witty, Sween and Connell stayed on the beach ignoring the heavy rain, the darker clouds and the wind kicking up. Fralhem was groaning and mumbling in his coma as the tide was rising near their beach shelters.

"Prestern! Charlie! Connell" They looked up and saw Canonchet.

"You all must gather what you can, and we must get to high ground. The storm's getting worse."

There was no hesitation. They took all bottles, empty or filled, in wooden crates, loosened the catch of crabs and fish in the rising tide and carried Fralhem on a stretcher.

When they left the beach, the wind got worse. It made one of the shelters collapse, and trees began to bend into arks like fishing rods. It blew off the laundry pinned on the line, and thunder started bombing like cannons.

The crew followed Canonchet near the hill, but they all stayed near the tree line since lighting had begun to flash and striking the hill spot. They all then sat tight around a robust, thick tree that couldn't bend.

Fralhem laid on the stretcher not bothered by the storm and was still not woken up.

Inside Fralhem's head.

In darkness and confusion again, Fralhem shouted, screamed and pleaded.

"What's going on? Get me out of here!"

With a blink of his eyes, he was in a room with two children. One looked older than the other, and they were all alone in a room full of small beds with bars on a window.

The older boy placed the small one on a bed and just walked out saying nothing.

"What is this?" Fralhem said to himself as he looked to the small child that was more of a baby.

The infant just sobbed and cried, but when Fralhem got closer, it's crying stopped. They baby open his eyes. Fralhem recognized them.

"Vilhelm!" He heard a woman's voice calling him by his real name. "Vilhelm!" Vilhelm, you abandoned your brother."

It was his mother.

Then he looked to the baby now grown into a young child in street rags.

The boy looked up with eyes of sadness and hate.

"You abandon me!" the boy yelled out loud.

The noise rang in Fralhem's ears making him scream in agony.

Back to the island.

The men and woman looked to the mate now screaming in his sleep.

"Christ what is wrong with him?!" asked Connell.

"He must be having a terrible nightmare!" replied Alasia.

"Or he's gone mad," said Sween.

Before the crew was to say more a lightning bolt struck the grassy meadow right in front of the tree just a yard away from the group. All jumped to their feet and ran back into the jungle, leaving the mate behind. And at the moment the flash struck, and Fralhem awakened.

"Kristoffer!"

All the crew heard the cry and ran back up for their mate.

"Oh no, my little bro…!" Fralhem rose from the ground and realized he could feel again which meant he was in the real world and finally awake.

"What? What's happening?" Fralhem said looking around with rain falling and the grass waving.

"Fralhem! Fralhem!" He knew it was Charlie. He got off the stretcher, but his legs were asleep making him walk wobbly.

"Charlie!" he replied, and the boy ran and embraced him.

"Thank God you're awake," Charlie said holding him up.

"Let's get to cover in the jungle! Come on!"

He led the dizzy officer to the group.

"Hey Fralhem's, awake!" shouted Witty. The cheering men were soon down since the storm was getting stronger, and the wind was blowing more strongly snapping a branch and nearly crashing down on the crew.

"We need to relocate to a safer area," said Sween.

"Follow me!" shouted Alasia. "There's a small cave to the southeast side."

The men all followed with Witty and Charlie helping the dizzy Fralhem gets across the windy jungle.

After making their way to a cave, they all cramped inside. Though it was dark, smelly and infested with rats, the crew remained in the small dry hole, where it was safe from the fallen trees, lighting and the rising tide.

CHAPTER 35

Washed Up

The storm cleared away hours later after the group had taken cover in a tiny rat cave. On the morning of the 9th of June, now 47 days being lost, most of the crew left the cave to stretch their limbs. Only Fralhem and Alasia remained in the tunnel.

While the others went out to see what had become of their shelters back on the beaches Fralhem was now ready to talk plainly again.

"So, I never had a chance to say last night but, Witty told me you and Evekins stayed and tended to me when I was out," said Fralhem. "And I thank you."

"Yes, you're welcome," Alasia said taking the mate's hand. "When you were out you made… a lot of strange noises and tossed around real violently. I take it you must've had a bad dream."

"Well it was something unpleasant, but I feel it was more than just a dream," replied Fralhem. Alasia wanted to ask but didn't want to pressure the man, and the two just sat quietly outside the open area of the cave watching the black clouds blow away down the horizon.

"Mr. Fralhem!" The mate heard and saw it was Witty calling him. The sailor walked over. "Well, sir I have good news and bad. The bad news is that the raft has been crushed by a tree and… uh."

"Yes," said Fralhem seeing Witty's deep hesitation to finish.

"Well, I think your gonna have to follow and see for yourself," the man replied.

Fralhem got up with Alasia walking him across the island and through the jungle with Witty leading the way.

They went out to the beach and found all of their shelters had been destroyed, washed up to the jungle line, but that was not what Witty wanted to show them.

After another walk passing the area where they camp,

Witty led them to an area of the rocky beach. And they saw it.

There along with the rest of the crew.

It was the young bull sperm whale. It had beached up on the shore with rope tangled all around its body along with bleeding scratches it had got from the coral rocks.

"The calf," Fralhem said as he and Alasia walked up to it.

"Can you believe this?" said Connell who turned to the mate. "And take a look on the other side."

Fralhem walked around and saw the whaleboat. "Min Gud! Our boat."

"Guess the whale took it, and now he's given it back to us," said Witty.

All the men gathered behind the mate staring at the boat next to the whale.

"Well, what are you all standing around for?" said Fralhem. "Let's take it!"

The six men walked up to the boat and as they held it by the sides, the whale awoke.

It vastly flapped its fluke splashing the men and soaking them, making them retreat to the rocks.

"What are you frightened of cowards?!" Fralhem yelled at the men. "It's helpless, and we're whalers."

The mate shook his head and walked up to the line

attached to the boat, bringing it away from the panicking whale.

"Well, come on help me! Idiots!" Fralhem ordered.

Canonchet, Charlie, and Connell came and helped the mate haul it on the land leaving the whale stuck on the rock bed.

They brought the boat to the stand beachhead where the shelters were.

The whale boat's lower hull was covered with layers of barnacle and it was missing a wooden plank on its port railing along with half the oar hooks.

"Connell? You think yee can fix her?" asked Fralhem.

"Aye captain, it's nothing I can't handle," he answered.

On the inside of the boat were wet hemp rope, a bucket, and a rusted lance.

"Alright, now Connell will fix the boat, Witty you'll assist him, Canny, Prestern reset the shelters, Charlie, Sween and Miss LaCapet fetch the water."

After Fralhem made the orders most of the crew went to their duties, he then reached down in the boat and picked up the lance.

"Where are you off to sir?" Witty asked.

"I'm going to put the calf out of its misery," the mate answered, then walked off. The crew all stared for a while, but just returned to their work.

CHAPTER 36

Secret Act of Mercy

Dusk came, now the end of another day, but the men felt so relieved now they had their boat back. Connell nailed new timber on the boat's rail side scrapped all the barnacles off and tightly secured a mast in the center from a thin tree that Witty cut down. Canonchet and Prestern rebuilt the shelter, and only Sween returned with all the water in the green Du Vin bottles.

"So, where's Charlie and Miss Alasia at?" asked Prestern as they sat around the fire.

Well, after they learned Fralhem went off to kill the whale they wanted to help or watch since Charlie had sparked the lady's interest in the whaling business.

"Ha ha, a woman has gone whaling," joked Connell.

Now dark came and the men sat eating fish and joking more about Charlie's affection for Alasia.

When they heard noises, they saw Fralhem had returned with Alasia and Charlie.

"Well I expected if you had killed the whale you'd be covered in blood," said Witty. Seeing not a stain on any of their clothes.

"Because we didn't," said Fralhem.

"Why what happ..." Before Connell could finish he was interrupted.

"It got away!" Yelled Fralhem wielding his lance as he walked into the jungle.

Then Charlie and Alasia sat in the fire circle.

"What happened?" Prestern asked.

"Well, we'd tell you, but you might not believe," answered Alasia.

"Tell us!" said Canonchet. "I'm up for a story."

"Well…Fralhem didn't kill the whale," answered Charlie. All men turned and looked to one another.

"Why?" Canonchet asked.

"A whaler showing mercy to a whale?" asked Sween surprised.

"Why? We asked him the same thing," said Alasia.

"When we finished gathering the water bottles we went off to see and when we got there…" Alasia paused and looked at Charlie.

"Well, Fralhem must have lost or had no intentions of killing the whale… He was trying to help it."

"A Whaler saving a whale?" asked Sween.

"He sure did," Charlie stated. "The tide rose up, and the whale was struggling to retreat back into the ocean, but it needed a push which was exactly what Fralhem did. With a few strong pushes he helped the whale swim away from the land."

"No way," said Connell.

"Well go see for yourself cause the whale is no longer on that rock beach," said Alasia.

That's not like Fralhem," said Witty. "Why would he do that?"

All sat puzzled around the fire until Canonchet sat up.

"Where are you going? asked Prestern.

"Have a word with him," he answered and then walked into the jungle.

CHAPTER 37

"Follow the Signs."

Canonchet walked through the moonlit jungle and found Fralhem up on the watch hill.

"Fralhem?" Canonchet called.

"Hello, Canny. What brings you up here?" he asked.

"Thought I'd give my captain some company," Canonchet replied. He sat on the log next to Fralhem who was just staring at the sky. Canonchet stared at him.

"So what's with you?" Fralhem asked becoming weary of his harpooner staring at him.

"I'm concerned," Canonchet answered. "Are you alright?"

"What's that supposed to mean?" Fralhem asked defensively.

"Come on Vilhelm. Charlie and Alasia saw you, and they told us you saved that whale and helped it escape. That's not your whaling skills. Why did you save it?" Canonchet asked.

"Oh Christ!" yelled Fralhem standing up, "Look if you're going to criticize me..."

"No, I'm not criticizing sir," said Canonchet. "Just tell me. Come on I'll listen."

"You'll think I've gone mad," said Fralhem.

"I've sailed with you for years," said Canonchet. "I trust you, I don't think you crazy, and you're still our captain… now tell me."

Fralhem sat back down and rubbed his head. "Alright, it's strange, but I will tell you."

Canonchet sat and listened. Fralhem told him everything about the strange dreams with the helpless whale calf being slain and his young brother all alone.

"Well, they sound like nightmares," said Canonchet.

"I know. It sounds ridiculous," replied Fralhem.

"Well, you didn't follow it, you did the complete opposite..."

"No, I didn't follow it," Fralhem interrupted. "I should have killed the whale and we would have plenty of meat."

"No, no, no, what I mean if you listened to what that dreamed showed you," explained Canonchet.

"Showed me what?" he asked.

"Well, you must have had a premonition; my wife has told me about them," Canonchet said. "They are dreams of a future, like Deja vu only a sight of what may or may not happen."

"If you've killed that whale you may never see your brother again. So you stopped that nightmare from coming true by sparing that calf and helping it back to the sea."

"Pure nonsense. Everyone would call me crazy," said Fralhem.

"Well, I don't, neither Charlie nor Alasia. And I'm sure Prestern will understand," Canonchet said patting his shoulder. "Just keep that in mind."

The mate looked to his shipmate with a relaxed smile.

"Well! I... ah we should place that all aside." Fralhem said changing the subject. "Now we have our boat back we can get off this spit of land. You should get some rest."

The native got up and walked back to the beach leaving the reassured mate up on the hill.

CHAPTER 38

"WE'LL MISS THE EDEN"

Eight days after the beached whale and the return of the boat, all was prepared, and the crew was now gathering more fresh water and provisions of salted fish to off the island. Which Charlie and Alasia were put up for that task by Fralhem to collect bottles of pond water.

It was now apparent to the whole crew that the couple had fallen for one another.

In the jungle at the freshwater pond. Charlie saw a worried look on Alasia's face.

"Are you scared?" he asked.

"A little," she answered. "It's been awhile since I've gone out to sea. Now I'm leaving the land that's been my home for years."

"You call this island home?" he asked. "Not that I blame you it is a beautiful speck of nature."

"It is," she replied looking in all directions. "It was like my own secluded island with no laws or troubled by other people. A hundred times better than that drafty house on Papeete. I even doubt I'll have that house back since my country never bothered to come searching for us."

"So, what will you do when we return to civilization?" he asked.

"I don't know, what will you do?" she asked back.

"I'm not sure," he answered looking down.

"You're not going back to whaling?" she asked.

"It's too dangerous and harsh for me," he replied.

"Well, I can understand… At least we have one another," she said smiling.

The two shared a kiss of passion and held hands as they went to the beach.

CHAPTER 39

DEPARTING

"We thank you, God, for giving of us refuge on this land you gave to Miss Alasia and to us as well," Prestern stated in a hand to hand prayer with the crew. "And we thank you for returning our vessel. We will depart this island of the sanctuary so that we can return home. We know you're watching us from above and we thank you for all you've given us."

"Amen," all said together like a chorus.

All boarded and sat in the usual positions, with Fralhem piloting the boat from the stern with the tiller at hand.

The rest took to the oars carved by Connell and began to row away from the island with a supply of dried fish, bird meat and 60 bottles of Du Vin filled with fresh water.

As they rowed off, Fralhem saw Alasia shedding some tears from her sockets. He thought of taking one last look back at the island, but he did not, believing it would make the rest feel worried.

"Now Sween hoist up the sail," ordered the mate.

Sween pulled the line on the single mast and up came a square sail pushed by the winds.

It was 18th of June and the castaway crew of the Mako was making their final push for New Zealand and return to the land of their home.

CHAPTER 40

Rescued

It was the 30th of July 1860 and weeks since the lost whalers had left the island. All the fish and bird meat had been devoured, every Du Vin bottle emptied. Over a month past and no sign of land or ship. Naked fish hooks dangled below in the open water, but no fish were caught. A tattered sail fluttering like curtains of a haunted house on the tree mast.

And the crew… The seven men and a woman lay helpless down in the boat now serving as their own sea coffin. They languished with thirst and hunger and thoughts of the loved ones they'd left behind, to be their last thoughts before leaving this world.

Canonchet hung his arm out over the bow looking at his reflection from the side, in the calm flat surface, with his index finger making ripples, as he saw visions of tickling one of his little ones.

Connell, behind the native, held Sween and Witty tight in his arms as he imagined them as his two twin sisters.

Charlie held his arm around Alasia, his face close to hers. She was gripping tightly on his hand.

To the end of the vessel, the ill Prestern sat against the knee of Mr. Fralhem.

The mate just sat upon his seat still gripping the boat's rudder, but he hung his head over the old steward. Images of his little brother danced in his head, and Prestern felt tears dripping on his head, but the old man didn't mind.

All seemed to have given up and were now at the end of

their long whale line. That's when a sound came to the ears of the crew; the sound of a steam whistle.

It awakened the people aboard the boat yet were too stiff to move.

Far below the hook lines, was the young bull whale swimming under the shadow of the boat. When it finally emerged for air, its spout soaked the crew, cooling the heat beating down on their dry bodies.

All began to move.

Canonchet got on his knees to look, Charlie sat up and turned, and Connell released his two friends who all sat up to see what was out there past the whale… It was a ship.

The chocked Canonchet turned to his languished shipmates, "A ship…coming… we're saved…" the man said in a dry whisper-like voice.

Prestern sat up. "Mister Fralhem…Mister Fralhem," the old men tried to yell in his sour voice. He put his hand on the mate's back and shook him.

"Wake up…boy, we made it."

Fralhem slowly opened his eyes and, sat up straight with creaks and cramps coming from the joints of his bones. He looked….and saw a giant ocean liner coming straight at them.

Prestern looked to the mate now trying to stand. Fralhem lifted his body from the seat and the old steward could hear cracks, snapping from the legs.

When Fralhem stood up straight, he lifted his arm. The boat sounded its horn.

And all survivors on the whaleboat smiled with tears of joy, knowing the ship had spotted them and their misery was finally at an end.

Prestern loosened his grip on the mate's leg. Fralhem

lost his balance and fell backward off the boat and, straight into the sea.

All turned but didn't have the strength to look if Fralhem was keeping himself out of the water. Their mate was overboard, and they heard no lack of splashes or attempts at trying to stay above water.

"No," Canonchet sickly yelled.

CHAPTER 41

On the whale's snout

"Bring the longboat down!" an officer shouted. Passenger came out leaving their breakfast to watch the crew rescue the drifting boat full of castaways as the liner's lifeboat came down and rowed alongside the faded whaler.

They noticed the castaways were trying to tell them something, but they didn't bother to try to understand and made their way back to the Tracy.

Fralhem's eyes began to go dark, and he drew his last breath with a large bubble leaving his mouth as he sank into the depths not being able to swim or move.

A strong push took him back to the surface that felt big and hard like a smooth rock. The sound of clicks sounded in Fralhem's ears.

They breached the surface. Fralhem drew breath and coughed out water, realizing what had saved him from drowning. The water shot out behind him.

"Look!" a child passenger shouted, "a whale!" Every passenger was shocked and surprised. "And a man!" yelled another. "A man on a whale's nose."

"Shiver, my soul it is," said the officer.

The crew on the lifeboat saw the passengers point behind them. "Jesus and Mother,

Mary...Look at that!"

They turned and saw the bull whale with Fralhem laying on the tip of the whale's round, scarred head. It swam close up to the boats just a foot away from the oars.

A sailor aboard quickly looped a line around Fralhem and pulled him aboard.

"Grab him," the mate shouted.

The weak whalers laying down on the lifeboat seats realized the New Zealand crew had caught something. When they saw them pull up a man out of the water, all smiled and cried in joy. Their Captain Fralhem was the last to be rescued, finally, just when they thought he was gone forever.

From the vessel deck, the passengers crowded around to get a glimpse of the dried near-dead castaways. The liner's captain, George Buster, came down from the steering.

"So, what have we got here, Forey?" who was tending the starving boatmen.

"Well, ah eight people sir," Forey answered. "In quite bad condition; must have been drifting for weeks on a whale boat."

"Whaler's ay? Well it's a damn good thing we crossed them, or they wouldn't have lasted another day," he said looking at the man that they rescued from the whale's head.

"And I'm sure there will be quite a seafaring tale to spread."

When all seven whalers and the island girl were brought inside, Buster made rooms, clothes, and food ready for them.

CHAPTER 42

The RMS Tracy

Fralhem opened his eyes and woke on a clean, soft cot in a white-painted cabin with a golden stain window seal. A scent caught his nose.

He turned and saw a tray on the dresser next to him.

The mate tried sitting up to reach for it but was too weak, when a stewardess came in.

"Oh, thank goodness you're awake!" she said excitedly.

She left for a moment than later returned. She came up to Fralhem's bedside. She uncovered the tray of hot food and fed Fralhem. The starving man wanted to scarf it all down, yet he let the lady feed him like an infant.

When the man had enough to eat, he found the will to speak.

"Charlie, Canonchet, Prestern?" he asked the woman.

"Where are they?"

"Don't you worry sir. They're all safe, being tended to this very moment," she answered, now feeding him plum pudding.

"Well, can I ask what ship this is, ma'am?" he asked licking his lips for the taste.

"Of course," Before she answered, in came the captain.

"Ah Captain, sir," the stewardess said. "I'll let the captain speak with you and bring back tea."

"Thank you, Ruth," said the captain closing the door.

"Well, when I received the news you had awoken, I got here as soon as I could," the man said shaking Fralhem's bony hand.

"Captain Buster is my name sir, Captain of Her Majesty's Royal Mail Ship Tracy of Wellington."

"Fralhem," he replied. "Third mate of the whaleship Mako from Nantucket. Been lost at sea since April. Might I ask where exactly did you pick us up?"

"About 60 miles west off the coast of Northland," the captain replied. "You were all really close to land yet when we found you were all close to death. Were you all set adrift aboard that old whaleboat the whole time?"

When Ruth the stewardess returned with the tea,

Fralhem told the two the story about being hauled away by the calf, to leaving the island.

From the other rooms, the other rescued whalers were being tended, and all told the story to their Stewards and Stewardesses. Soon the story was spread throughout the whole ship. Stewards told sailors, sailors told officers and officers said the passengers of what the eight people on the whaleboat had gone through.

After a week in their cabins, all the castaways were reasonably fed giving new clothes and fresh haircuts and shaves. They all reunited on deck.

"Well, sir we made it," Prestern said to Fralhem.

"Yes, we did," Fralhem said to his men. "Well we'll be alright aboard this fine vessel."

Captain Buster informed Fralhem that the ship was headed to Hawaii and he had already sent a telegram to New Zealand and Australia to send word back to America of their rescue.

"So, I'm sure your loved ones will be so thrilled to learn that you all have made it," Fralhem said patting Sween's shoulder.

"And it was all because of you sir," Connell said shaking

Fralhem's hand. "You were right, and I was wrong, sorry I doubted you."

"Guess we'll be famous when our story reaches home," said, Witty.

"Yes, indeed it will." All turned and saw a well-dress first class passenger.

"Your story quite opened my mind," said the man wearing a fancy suit and top hat. "Never can imagine men would go through such hardship."

"And you are, sir," asked Sween.

"Simon Horatio of Liverpool," He answered. "I would like you all to join me for dinner this evening, it would be my treat."

All agreed to finally have dinner in a public area rather in their cabin like prisoners.

CHAPTER 43

A Proposition

That evening on the last day of July, the castaway crew dined in the ship's restaurant where, other first-class passengers were seated, and an orchestra played fancy music.

"My, my, my, most of my life I've served white boys, and I think this is the first time a white waiter served me," said Prestern who ordered a jumbo shrimp cocktail with grits.

"You said it brother this food reminds of Louisiana," Witty replied enjoying oyster sauce with pasta.

The group enjoyed their meals eating food they hadn't eaten in years. Canonchet had veal cutlets and sweet potatoes, Connell had a shepherd's pie with corn beef, Sween ate chicken and rice, Charlie had banger and mash, Alasia ate eggs and bagels, and Fralhem had buttered cod and caviar.

Throughout dinner everyone just enjoyed themselves. Mr. Horatio who sat in the center of the table said little either, but he looked as though he wanted to speak.

The man really expected the people to talk about their voyage of being lost at sea, being marooned and the young whale, but none ever spoke of it. When dinner was nearly over Horatio finally found his voice to start a conversation.

"So, you are all American whalers? Yes?" he asked.

"Well no, I am," Canonchet said chewing on a veal slice.

"Ja and since I'm the lowest ranking officer I would get foreigners, African and Native Americans," replied Fralhem in agreement.

"While the higher ones get all white," said Witty.

"Can't wait to see the faces on the rest of the Mako crew when we make it back."

Horatio really did not want to talk of their planes to get home; he really wanted their story. So, when they had all finished their dinner. Horatio spoke up again.

"So, I'll be happy to buy you all desert, but would you all be so bold to share me your survival story?" he asked in an impatient tone and all stared at their host.

"So that's what you're after?" asked Sween. "Want us all to recount, the hell we've been through?"

Horatio looked down and nodded like a shy child.

"Count me out," Canonchet said getting out of his chair.

"Me too," said Witty. "Once is enough.

When the two men stood, Horatio got up.

"Wait! Please… don't get me wrong," he said sitting them back down. "Please, I don't mean to push you all…

How about after dessert? You all can at least think about it and give me an answer yes or no."

All looked to one another and agreed.

At the end of the dessert, Horatio now asked who was ready to share their story.

"Very well," said Fralhem. "I'll tell it."

"I'll come too," said Connell. Prestern stood and shook his head.

The rest just left for their quarters below.

The three followed Horatio to his private promenade deck where a small table with cigars and brandy was placed.

When they were seated around, Mr. Horatio he took a pen a notepad and Connell began the story. Prestern filled in parts Connell would miss, like when he doubted Fralhem and being restrained.

While the two chatted and smoked cigars, Fralhem was sipping on the brandy.

Horatio listened and took in as much as he could fit on the blank pages on his pad. Yet as it went on, both Connell and Preseten got really drunk, and the man was having difficulties understanding them.

Soon Prestern passed out on Connell's shoulder and Connell just mumbled on different stories about his past life in Ireland and nothing about being lost at sea.

Soon the annoyed Horatio lost his interest and looked at Fralhem who had said nothing the whole time.

"Well, if you are drunk I will have my servant help you back to your cabins," he said.

"No bother, I'm not drunk sir," Fralhem replied, "I'll tell ye the rest." Fralhem stood and went with Horatio inside while Horatio's servants put blankets on the two passed out men.

"You will have to excuse my men," Fralhem said. "Been too long since we had a taste of liquor. Before we finish off, why do you want our story? Make a book out of it? Or put it in the press?"

"Well, kind off," said Horatio. "You see I'm no writer but as businessmen."

"What kind of business?" Fralhem asked.

"I'm a shipbuilder, engineer, and a dock owner," he answered.

"And you want our story?" he asked a bit confused.

"I want the world to know what you have accomplished,

Fralhem." Horatio said. "You saved your men, and a whale saved you. A tale that can really turn a person's mind. A beast that was victim to humans and instead of taking revenge it helped the humans survive; it's unbelievable."

"I know I too find it hard to believe," Fralhem said sipping another glass.

"I believe it," Horatio said. "Because I saw it like many other passengers, some of them will spread the gossip."

"Yeah and will probably rewrite it," said Fralhem.

"Change our names, turn our story into a fairytale."

"I won't let that happen, I have a sister whose husband is connected with great novel writers," said Horatio. "Now please, I will pay you and your men good money, enough to buy you all another passage back home and to cover the time you lost away from your whaler. And that's my word."

Fralhem stared, a bit drunk yet his mind was obvious to understand and realized how insanely fair he was to him and his crew.

"Alright, let us finish this sea tale," Fralhem said taking another drink.

CHAPTER 44

A JOYFUL REUNION

On the first of October, The Tracy stopped at Honolulu. The seven lost whalers of the Mako once again step foot on the beautiful Hawaiian Islands.

Fralhem shook hands with Mr. Horatio in a farewell with a large amount of money in his pocket and the Liverpool shipbuilder with the story in his paper bag. After another handshake, they went their separate ways.

Fralhem brought shelter for his crew in a sailor's inn near the harbor.

To their surprise, they found no American sailors nor a tradesman, nor whaler.

When days past by not a single vessel had an American flag waving about.

When Fralhem asked foreign ship captain's and Hawaiian dock masters they gave no clear answer. Yet none of Fralhem's men were too worried about the matter, thinking some ships from their country would show up.

One beautiful autumn morning Charlie thought it be romantic to take Alasia out for a walk along the beach which she was pleased to do.

While walking on passed native Hawaiians, sailors, fishers and other beach dates, Charlie heard someone call for him.

"Can you hear that?" he asked.

"Yes, someone is calling your name," she replied.

"Can't be Fralhem," he said. "Sounds like a kid." They looked around to see who it was.

"Charlie! Charlie Evekins!" shouted Jethro Heszits running up waving his hand.

"Jeth?!" he shouted. "OH my God Jeth Heszits!"

He ran to the boy and embraced. "My God, Jeth how did you get here?"

"Signed on another vessel and jumped off again," the boy answered. "I heard that they were Nantucket whalers and when I heard an officer was of Norwegian I had to look for you guys. So, is the Mako docked here again?"

"We got a lot to tell you," Charlie introduced Jeth to Alasia and took him to the inn where the others were staying.

They all told Jeth their story of being lost at sea for a hundred days when a sperm whale hauled their boat away.

CHAPTER 45

ONGOING

By the 7th of January 1861, Fralhem's crew now wanted off Hawaii and to go back home. There were still no ships headed to the east coast of America. Some trade ships were heading to San Francisco, but the crew did not want to go, thinking it would take too long and they feared to cut across the western territories with hostile natives. They would much rather stick to the ships that would take them straight to New England.

On the first week of the year, Fralhem finally managed to fix a one-way passage to North America on a Peruvian fishing ship that would take them to Mexico.

So now with Jethro in his crew, they sat cramped in a storage area with reeking fish right below the Peruvian crew, who had better quarters.

"Well, how do we like that? We were once aboard a luxurious ocean liner and now we're once again poor people," said Witty.

"Easy things go so quickly," said Connell. "Hardship will always be around every corner of life."

"Look at the bright side brothers," said Prestern. "We are getting closer and closer to home."

On the 30th of March, after months sitting with dry salted fish, the Peruvian captain dropped Fralhem's crew on a Mexican beach at Oaxaca.

In Mexico, the country was twisting in a tied of a War of Reform, between the Libraries and the conservative government. So, they got little to no help from the Mexican authorities who were tied up in the conflict. They had to fend for themselves.

From word of locals and Mexican Rebels, Fralhem learned of American ships off the Mexican coast. He purchased some mules, a two-wheel cart wagon and now the crew made way to the Atlantic coast of the gulf.

"It's nice to see such beautiful countryside," Sween Said to Canonchet, admiring the Mexican jungle valley.

"And yet this was all once part of the mighty Aztec empire."

"That was all wiped out," Canonchet said smoking a new pipe. "Just like my fellow Algonquians."

"Well yes, but not completely," Sween said. "Your tribe still lives around their old areas in New England, just under Whiteman law."

"Yes, that's true," Canonchet replied. "We still long for the past though, live the way we want. Yet what you said, we are being persecuted, but we won't be forgotten. Can we talk about something else?" he pleaded.

"Yeah, you're right," Sween said riding a mule. "Well, we're passing through the thin part of the land from one sea to another and we whalers, all sailing in the world always have to sail around the Cape Horn of South America. They should find some place in the narrowest part of the land in Central America and make a pass way for ships."

"Sounds impossible," said Canonchet. "Away for ships sounds like a good plan, to make cargo shipment much easier."

"Yep and the use of ground oil, new machines, new constructions," Sween added.

"Oh yes. No more long voyages, no whale hunting and no adventures," Canonchet said.

"Well, not now but maybe when we're old and gray," said, Sween.

"Yeah let us hope so," Canonchet replied.

Four weeks later, April 27, it had now been over a year since they'd been lost. Fralhem's crew made it to the Mexican Gulf coast. When they entered the first port, they learned not a single vessel was from America, nor was any Mexican ship heading to the States.

On a dockyard of Coatzacoalcos, Fralhem with Sween went to the dockmaster. When asked, it was always, "No ships are going to America."

And when Fralhem asked, "Are there any American ships expected to come dock here?" the dock masters replied in Spanish.

Fralhem saw that Sween had a look of confusion and discomfort.

Words were exchanged back and forth. Sween ended the conversation with "gracias."

"Well, any word on the next ship from America coming?" he asked Sween, who was looking down like someone had died.

"No. No ships from America will be coming and not anytime soon," the man answered.

When words came to the rest of the crew all were disappointed and upset at the news.

"You mean not a single vessel will take us to America, nor is any American ship coming?" asked Prestern.

"Yes, the dockmasters and even other ship captains say so. And that's a fact because of the war going on and a blockade blocking all Southern ports..."

"Whoa! Whoa! Slow down there Sween," said Connell.

"Remember we haven't been reading the newspapers

lately, and we've been lost at sea for a while. So what war and what blockade is that exactly?"

"They said The U.S. Navy is blocking almost every port in the south, all the way from Galveston, Texas to Washington D.C."

"Wait why is The U.S. Navy blocking its own ports?" asked Charlie.

"America is at war," said Sween. "And it turns out it's not united."

"Oh, for God's sakes! No riddles, bookworm! Get to the point!" demanded Connell. "Who is America at war with?!"

"Itself," Sween answered. "Our country is now at war with itself. It's a civil war and looks to be quite a major one."

"Guess we have to travel by land," said Canonchet.

"Might take longer but with no other resource, no other choice."

"Yeah, guess you're right," Fralhem said.

CHAPTER 46

Favor for a Favor

Outside a Mexican tavern a few days later. Fralhem brought drinks for the crew. Now they were making plans on how to get to America. Since Mexico and their country was at war, they expected the worst and thought it would take much longer for them to get home.

To their surprise, a man came to their table.

"Americans? "the Mexican gentleman said, with an elder one behind. All looked a bit puzzled.

"You Americans? From?" he asked.

"Americanons. Si," replied Sween, realizing the men were trying to ask them something.

So Fralhem had Sween sit down with the Mexican men.

After sharing a few drinks and chatting in Spanish. Sween returned to the crew all smiles.

"Well my friends, guess we do not have to travel north, we can make sail for home."

"They're gonna take us to Nantucket?" asked Charlie.

"Well not exactly, but halfway," Sween replied. He sat with the rest of the crew and told them everything that the Mexican captain had offered him.

"Captain Altorga of the skipper "El Teolacho," said he heard of American whalers in need of passage to America," explained Sween. "Now he said he won't take us as far north as New England but will drop us off at Florida since he's sailing to Havana. And he needs some experienced sailors to help."

Fralhem and Sween walked over to Captain Altorga and his man.

"Mr. Sween, tell the captain we will go with him, it's a fair deal."

After Sween translated. Fralhem stuck out his hand, and Altorga shook it.

CHAPTER 47

The Iron passage

Early in May, two weeks after leaving Mexico on a crafty old schooner, the El Teolacho came across a Union Naval vessel.

The USS Retriever, off the coast of the Florida Keys.

Altorga signaled the vessel and the two ships came close to one another. Fralhem's crew boarded the iron steamship and shook hands in farewell with the old captain, finally on a ship to take them home.

Two more weeks passed as they sailed north passing by dozens of other Naval fleets that are blocking major Southern ports like Savannah, Charleston, and Norfolk. For the passengers there was no question that this civil war in America was bloody.

On the 30th of May, the Retriever dropped the castaways in the harbor of Annapolis. Fralhem's crew finally stepped foot on their home country's soil after a long three years.

Smiles cut onto the men's faces as they were drawing nearer and nearer to home.

It crossed their minds to write letters, yet they didn't want to take the time. They just wanted to plot a straight on course home to their families.

When they came into the nation's capital, Washington D.C., the streets were flooded with tens of thousands of blue-uniformed men. The armies were so vast it brightened the whalers' eyes with amazement.

They boarded a train that would take them to Springfield, Massachusetts.

At the station seeing more and more carts carrying hundreds of soldiers, horses, cannons, and supplies fit for an island population all coming down from every Northern state of the Union. More shocking was when they read the newspapers about the massive army enlistments called by the new President Abraham Lincoln. They also had heard of the conflict that was to end slavery and secession, but they would never have thought it would lead to such a bloody conflict.

Still, they wanted to be embraced by their loved ones and worry about what's happening another time.

CHAPTER 48

ACKNOWLEDGMENT

On June third, the train arrived in Springfield. Here Fralhem disbanded his crew.

"Well… we made it men," He said. "I kept my promise to take you home. Now I want you all to go. Go to your wives, children, brothers, sister, and parents. I will find out what has come of our ship the Mako and I will do what I can, to have the ship owners send you your profits."

All the men felt a bit sadder now leaving their leader, yet all the same, they were so eager to leave. They shook Fralhem's hand one by one and went their separate ways.

Connell returned to his sisters, Witty to his mother and siblings in Boston. Prestern went home to his daughter and granddaughter. Canonchet went home to his wife and children back in Connecticut, same for Sween.

Only Jethro, Charlie and Alasia remained.

"Mr. Fralhem? May we come along with you?" asked Alasia. "Just to see if you need any help."

Fralhem wanted to object but decided not to and let them come along.

In the whaling capital port of New Bedford, the group walked through the streets near the big dockyards to find dozens of whaleships docked and closed, some even being stripped for scrap. Not only were the ships anchored but the ship repair houses were shut down, oil warehouses empty and long lines of sailors stretched out for miles crowding the sidewalks to enlist in the Union Navy and Army.

More disappointment ran through the heads of the

castaways, realizing how much they've missed and that the nation they had lived and worked for was being torn apart. Now discovery the war was destroying the lucrative whaling industry.

So they entered into the whaling inquiry headquarters of the ship owners. Naval officers were now using it and an officer that pointed out where the ship owners were currently working.

When they entered, there was only one man going through the captain's logs of returned whalers, with the last barrels of oil now taken by the Union army.

"Not as great as it once was," Fralhem said sitting in front of the man.

"I suppose you're a returned whaler?" The man said.

"Well, yes, but I'm not the captain," he replied.

"Well, what the hell are you coming into my office for huh?" the gentleman replied real aggressive. "If you want a ship, they're all docked, and we're closed for the time being."

Soon other ship owners entered the office with paperwork and sat next to the table.

"This war has truly taken a toll on you whalers,"

Fralhem responded.

"Who is this man?" the second owner asked.

"I asked, and he won't answer," the first one replied.

"My name is, Mr. Fralhem," he answered. "I'm here because I need information about a Nantucket whaleship Mako; I tried getting a ride to the island, but no one would take me, so here I am."

"The Mako? The second owner replied. "Captain Calais Gerard's ship?"

"Yes, the son of our former partner Henry Gerard," the third owner recalled.

"Yes, I remember him," the first owner said, now looking to Fralhem. "The Mako… is gone."

Fralhem was astounded, and his face turned pale.

"What happened."

"Well. By the first mate's account, it happened three months ago. The Mako was homeward bound when Gerard brought the ship into a squall. He and near half the crew was lost along with the Mako herself."

"The first, second mate and less than half a dozen other survivors were picked up, and the account was brought here to New Bedford when word got to Nantucket. Gerard's father resigned," said the third owner.

"So that's what happened," said the first. "Now why…"

Before they could ask, Fralhem got out of his chair and stormed out of the building.

"Evekins, Heszits, come we're leaving," he said.

"Where are we going?" Charlie asked.

"To Branter's manor," he answered.

CHAPTER 49

AN APOLOGY

Fralhem brought a carriage, and the others rode in the back.

"So, Mr. Branter made it home?" asked Jethro.

As Fralhem and the others rode on, he told them what the owners had told him.

He made it to Branter's home on the outskirts of New Bedford.

There they saw other carriages parked on the front yard of the house.

The four came up to the front door and knocked. After a while. It was answered by Branter's wife, Pearl.

"You're not Tisburn," she said.

"Oh Mrs. Branter, you don't remember me?" Fralhem asked.

Before she could reply he said, "Come now, your husband had me over for supper sometimes, and I served with him. I started as a harpoo…" Before he finished, Peral Branter recalled, with a surprised expression on her face.

"Oh my God, Mr. Fralhem!" she stated nearly in tears.

She immediately let him and the others inside. Soon after Tisburn came in, to find his long-lost shipmate.

The two shipmates embraced.

"God damn you Fralhem. How the hell are yee on this gloomy day to brighten it up!" shouted Tisburn. Mrs. Branter soon hushed it. "And you Evekins and Jeth, where were you all?"

They quickly shared their story with the mate, Branter's wife, and housemaid. As soon as they finished, the group now wondered why so many carriages were outside, and what has become of Branter.

The former second mate looked to the lady who nodded.

"Well… them carts out there belong to doctors." Tisburn explained.

All were now worried.

"Is Branter alright?" asked Jethro.

Mrs. Branter was called up by a nurse.

"Not good I'm afraid," answered Tisburn, as they sat in the dining room downstairs drinking coffee. Tisburn soon filled them in with the details.

"We discovered a fire in the oil hold.

We manage to escape in the boats, but that idiot Gerard and other crewmen like Timrod stayed thinking they could save the ship, but they just wanted to save the stuff that would pay them.

Branter was really wise when we got a distance from the vessel. The Mako blew up… it was so huge and bright as if a piece of the sun had hit the water, and it nearly swamped us. We survived, but we returned home with no ship, no oil, and no pay. Branter caught himself a fever, and it has been giving him the devil ever since. Guess your story is a bit better than ours."

"Never mind that," said Fralhem. "I'm glad you men made it… just want to see Branter."

"Fralhem?" Pearl came down with tears in her eyes.

"Isaac is awake…and wants to see you… and Jethro."

The two stood up and followed the lady of the house.

The upstairs hallway was crowded with doctors and two butlers.

In the master bedroom, the two heard Mrs. Branter talking. A doctor and nurse walked out, then the former third mate and cabin boy went in.

They saw the wife over their first mate, a middle-aged Isaac Branter, who now looked as though he was in his 70s with gray hair, pale skin wrinkles, and a long straggly beard.

"Here they are my love," she said. "It's not a dream, they made it."

When she helped the man look up, Branter's eyes brighten as though he had seen an angel.

"Fralhem...Jeth... my dear shipmates..." Branter expressed in a weak voice and a few coughs.

The two slowly walked over to the man's side.

"Pearl my darling. Let them come," he said to his wife.

When she cleared the way, the two took Branter's bony hands.

"I can't believe this. I didn't believe it, "he said.

"Believe it, sir," said Jethro. "It's true we are here, we made it."

"You did," Branter said beginning to shed tears.

"Your boat? Fralhem?" he asked concern.

"Yes sir," the third mate reassured. "Prestern, Canonchet, Sween all of my men we all made it."

When he heard the men, he thought were lost were alive all along, Branter began to sob. Pearl came to his other side.

"Isaac, it's alright..." she tried to calm him.

"No it's not!" he shouted. "Mr. Fralhem and his men suffered and it's all my fault."

"Oh, sir please don't stress yourself," said Fralhem.

"It's my fault Fralhem; I left you behind! I gave up on you! When your boat never returned, I didn't bother to search for you, and I gave you up." Branter confessed, sobbing harder, as he began to cough deeper. "I don't deserve forgiveness...." Branter coughed more, and the two men gave him some room.

"Doctor come in here!" Pearl called out. "And Cole!

Make yourself useful and open the windows! Don't expect the servants to do everything."

They turned and saw Branter's teenage son who had been sitting in the corner the whole time.

When he opened a window, he said he'd be downstairs.

Pearl didn't hear but was helping the doctor getting medicine down Branter who was still coughing.

When Branter was calmed and settled down in the thick pillows. Fralhem and Jethro came back to his side.

"My wife…" called Branter. "Go with Cole… and please don't be so hard with him…" She wanted to stay with her husband, yet she did not want to argue, so she left with the doctor. Then Branter turned to his two shipmates. "I do not blame you if you all hate me…My suffering is justice."

"No Branter we don't," Before Fralhem finished, his shipmate cut him off.

"You would have made a much better captain than me," he said in a wheezing voice. "I don't deserve that rank… you made it safely along with your men and you, Jethro; I'm sure you'll be a great sailor than I was."

"Branter…" Jethro said beginning to cry.

"I now want to tell you two. And tell the rest of your crew, Fralhem." Branter paused a moment, trying to fight the pain, then spoke out. "I never knew such great whalers…

Great sailors…Great men. Now please go."

Fralhem shook his head and walked Jethro out the room.

When they exited, they had the nurse go back in. When they came down to the dining room, they saw Cole comforting his mother.

CHAPTER 50

Cremation

Throughout the day in Branter's home, they sat at the long dining table. Tisburn and Fralhem went outside to smoke their pipes on the back porch. Inside the house, Charlie and Alasia shared their story with Pearl, and the house servants while Cole played chess with Jethro. All tried to keep calm and steady while the doctors tended the dying chief mate.

The gloomy afternoon turned dark. Mrs. Branter had the servants prepared supper for the guest and doctors and just when they had a prayer at the table.

"Mrs. Branter! Mrs. Branter!" yelled the nurse. "You must come."

Everyone's appetite was gone, as the lady stood up and begun to run upstairs, with Cole following. The mates,

Charlie, Alasia, and Jethro paused and did not touch a morsel on their plates.

No one spoke, no one made any noise as voices came from upstairs. The only sound below was the sparks from the fireplace and the ticking from the mantle clocks.

They then heard a woman scream.

All knew it. A doctor came downstairs and whispered to one of the butlers.

The servant approached the table.

"Oh Mr. Fralhem, Tisburn…I'm sorry to tell you this… but Master Branter is…gone."

Tears welled out of Jethro's eyes.

Though she knew little of her lover's first officer, Alasia too began to shed tears.

"We survived a near death, and we went through so much... only to return and lose a friend," Charlie said in his mind embracing his weeping lover.

Fralhem just dropped his head on the table, after he pushed his plate of food away.

Two weeks later.

June 18th, 1861. Slowly walking on a long wooden dock, sticking out towards a light stormy sea of the bay of Cape Cod, walked the widow Pearl Branter and preacher Father Chappel with the vase carrying the ashes of the first mate Isaac Branter.

They came to the rear end of the dock. Widow Pearl went to her knees. The priest handed her the vase. She took it in her arms as if it was a baby.

Tears melted down her face as she slowly poured the ashes of her husband in the sea.

To the rear end were the mourners. Branter's son Cole, with close relatives and old shipmates. Fralhem, Tisburn, and Jethro.

After the widow returned to her son, all went their ways.

CHAPTER 51

Gossiping in an uncaring world

The surviving whalers of Fralhem's whaleboat were now back to their own lives on land.

Harpooner Canonchet returned to his loving family in Gordon, Connecticut. He tried several times to go back aboard whaling ships, but many whalers were too frightened to sail out since whale oil was a prime target for Confederate Navy and blockade runners. Even the Union Navy themselves would attack them to avoid the enemy from capturing valuable oil cargo.

He was approached a few times by army recruiters, but he always turned them down. So Canonchet turned to what he had started with, fishing. There were times when the man had money to spare, and he would go out for some drinks at the tavern, telling his story to Naval sailors and his fellow tribesmen. At one time when a drunk called the story rubbish, they get into a violent brawl which left him in jail.

After the funeral of Branter. Jethro said farewell to Fralhem and Charlie once again and went off to join the Navy aboard an iron gunship.

Owen Sween tried on several occasion to join the Union Navy as a midshipman, but the Admiralty thought he had no command instincts, and they rejected him. So, with the help of his father, he got a commission as a junior officer for a general's staff in Washington D.C. Sween tried his best to share out what he had gone through with Fralhem and the crew, yet none would care to listen since everyone was too concerned about the war. His family was thrilled of the life experience he went through, and they encouraged him to write about.

When Sween made a lengthy manuscript of his sea tale, it was turned down by every publisher he went to, from Boston to Washington.

Old Tom Prestern was now retired. He didn't go back to work as a cook nor a house servant. He dedicated himself to motivational speeches and became a church pastor. His inspirations from Douglas and Tugman made him join in Civil Right movements to encourage more enlistments of Black men for the Union forces.

And when he had time the old pastor tried to share the sea adventure he went on. Only his family believed him. While many others thought it was just a fairytale.

The carpenter, Kevin Connell, stayed out of the war and got a job building log homes around the New England wilderness. And like Canonchet he too drifted into alcoholism and spent a bit of time in jail for starting drunken brawls.

Connell tried to forget the story and rarely spoke of it to anyone. His sisters were shocked their brother had survived his time out at sea, so they shared the story for him.

Sam Witty and his family were facing bad money problems. His younger siblings had to be put in a workhouse, fixing sewing machines and making uniforms for the army.

He thought at first to join the Union navy since they allowed African Americans to serve, yet his mother didn't want him not to as he'd been away from his family way too long.

Fralhem went with Tisburn back to New Bedford to

discuss getting money sent to the surviving crewmembers of the Mako. With the assistance of Branter's father-in-law,

Fralhem kept his promise to send some of the salaries to his boat crew. At the end of the year 1861, with the war continuing and getting bloodier by the day, Tisburn decided to leave to join the Union Navy.

Fralhem avoided conscript and was living in a boarding house, working from job to job as a clerk, a cooper, fishermen, and a chimney sweeper. Doing everything he could to earn more money because he made a significant decision.

On Christmas eve in the boarding house, Fralhem had a visitor. It was a postman who had a letter for him.

When he opened it, was a wedding invitation, that read.

"Dear Vilhelm "Fralhem" Membjorg.

We request the honor of your company to attend the wedding of Alasia LaCapet and Charlemagne Evekins this 30th of December.

We would be eternally pleased to have you as our guest."

After he finished reading. Fralhem laughed real hard making other boarding guests stare at him.

"I'm off to a wedding!" he said to one of the tramps, with his hammock sack on his shoulder.

CHAPTER 52

WEDDING

In the half-empty church in Boston, the groom stood near Father Chapple looking down on the guests that had shown up.

Widow Pearl Branter had paid for the wedding ceremony.

She sat in the front row next to her senator father who helped legalize the marriage. Other relatives of the Branter family sat alongside them.

Behind them was Sween's family. In the other stalls next to them sat Connell with his two sisters Debbie and Denies and their children. Their husbands couldn't come since they'd joined the Army. Right behind was Witty who had brought his family. Prestern couldn't go because he was moving to New York.

The groom, Charlie was a bit disappointed because he wanted all the men he'd survived with to attend.

Especially Fralhem who still hadn't shown up.

"Hey! Worry not, old friend," his best man Cole Branter said patting his back. "He'll pop up eventually."

The organ played the bridal song. All stood up, and the groom turned. To see a real surprise:

Fralhem was walking Alasia down the aisle.

"Told you so," Cole jokingly said.

The sight brightened the hearts and souls of all the guests. They stopped thinking about the war and the castaways put aside all their problems as though it was a day of total world peace.

The ceremony was held at the Branter's summer house

in Plymouth. Fralhem was greeted by the grateful family members of his crew with big thank yous' and kisses' as if he was a war hero. During that time he discovered Cole and Charlie had developed a friendship and had got him a steady paid job in a telegraph station, where they wrote and transcribed essential messages from cargo ships.

Throughout the celebration, Fralhem just sat in the corner drinking wine as he watched the guests chat, dance and children play out in the snow.

Connell and Witty tried to strike up a conversation with their former boat officer, but Fralhem was too quiet and would only reply using a few words.

CHAPTER 53

The Decision

Later that evening Alasia and Charlie were about to leave for their honeymoon out to a small cottage in the country. After they shook and hugged most of the guests, Charlie went over to Fralhem leaning against the porch with a big smile on his mustached face.

"Well, Charles, you're moving up in the world," said the mate sipping more wine.

"It's really all thanks to you. Vilhelm," said Charlie. "My wife thinks that name suits you the most. And she thanks you as well for all you have done for us and the others."

"And it's also really thanks to you Charlemagne," the man replied. "If not for your help, I wouldn't have found myself, and I wouldn't have made it. You helped me find a purpose to survive. Which is why I decided to go back to my homeland, Norway."

Charlie's eyes brightened. "To your brother?"

Before Fralhem could answer, he was interrupted by one of the servants.

"Master Evekins, your wife, is waiting for you."

"Oh yes thank you." He said to the butler. "We uh well, Vilhelm talk to me about it when I return, I'm happy you decided that." He took Fralhem's hand and said goodbye.

Then he went to the carriage and the newly wedded couple left.

Fralhem was the first guest to leave.

CHAPTER 54

DON'T WORRY JUST HOPE

A week after the honeymoon. Mr. and Mrs. Evekins came back to Plymouth. Cole gave Charlie a letter that was unmarked.

He opened it and read it through with his wife.

"Charlie. We served a whaling voyage, were lost at sea and made it out together. I would like to thank you for all you have taught me, and I know you, and the rest of my boat crew won't forget it as well. I write to you and hope you don't mind writing to the other men. I'm going back to Norway the coming Spring. As soon as I put my money together, I'll be leaving in March. You can find me at the train station I'm departing from. The Address is on the back of the letter.

If you can't make, well then Farewell my good friend. It has been a real honor sailing with you.

Sincerely. Vilhelm Membjorg."

"We have to go to him," Alasia said. "Before he leaves."

"Yes, you're right," he said.

"And the others, Prestern, Canonchet, all his boat crew must come to say goodbye," she recommended.

"You're absolutely right," Charlie replied, "I'm not sure with Sween. But I believe Prestern would show up. Well, let us make the arrangements. You send word to Witty, Connell, and Canonchet. I'll send word to Prestern and Sween. Hopefully, they can come."

On the 9th March 1862, Fralhem now had all his belongings of clothes and enough money for a train to take him to Canada and buy a passage to his native home of

Norway. Staying at an inn near Medford, he received a letter from Charlie that he and his Alasia will meet him at the station on the very day he leaves.

That morning he sat on the bench outside near the tracks waiting for his friend. But to his surprise, he saw Charlie with a large group of people, some with familiar faces. A little African American girl came up to him.

"Mister. Fralhem?" she asked.

"Yes, I am," he answered. The girl ran up and gave him a tight hug.

"Thank you!" she said, "Thank you for saving my granddaddy."

"See ya finally met my granddaughter." Prestern came up. "Dawn this is Mr. Fralhem. Mr. Fralhem this here is my granddaughter Dawn."

Fralhem immediately stood up and shook Prestern's hand.

"I never thought I'd see you here."

"You thought we'd let you leave with no goodbye?"

Canonchet asked.

"My God, my boat warrior, has come to?" he said so surprised.

"Same for my wife," Canonchet replied.

"Hello Frahlem," said Aleshanee. "It's an honor to meet you finally."

He kissed her hand and met the rest of Canonchet's children.

Sween showed up in his army uniform.

"I see you made to the rank of captain," Fralhem said with a salute.

"Oh no Mr. Fralhem please salute me not," Said Sween."If any of us deserves this rank, it's you. I was given this rank just for serving generals brandy and keeping their headquarters clean."

"So basically, you're an army maid," joked Connell. "But less fancy. Well, Fralhem, I would go with ya back to the old world, but America has more to offer."

"Well men, it's not because of the country, or the war.

It's just a personal manner." Fralhem felt his heart warmed as he looked at his shipmates and his eyes began to mist.

"Your gonna look for your brother," said Charlie.

"Yes."

"It's gonna be hard no telling where he could be," said Witty."

"I'm not concerned about that," said Fralhem sniffing with a tear.

"What are you worried about the?" asked Alasia.

"Well, I'm not worried that I won't find my brother. I'm worried that he won't forgive me," said Fralhem.

"Well let's hope he will," she replied.

"Thank you," He said. Then all heard the cry from the train's captain.

"All aboard!"

"Well my friends, I thank you so much for being here,"

Fralhem said getting onto his cart. He shook all his crew by the hand. "Goodbye, my crew and fare thee well. God bless you all!"

The train moved on as Fralhem waved goodbye. And the wave returned by his crew and their loved ones whose eyes all began to turn into tears as the train pulled far out of sight.

"Farvel, farvel mine venns," he whispered as he sat down in his seat cupping his face to hide his tears from the other passengers.

"That was a great man there," Canonchet said to one of his sons. And again, the lost whaleboat crew of the Mako went their own way again.

CHAPTER 55

RETRACING

Months past and Fralhem made his way to Halifax, Nova Scotia late in the Autumn. There he found a Canadian merchant ship bound for Scandinavia.

To save money, he requested the vessel's master that he could serve abroad temporarily as a common sailor, to get home. At first, the ship's captain and officers were reluctant to except, but when he informed them of his experience on whaling ships and he'd serve aboard for free, they agreed to take him on.

The small trade ship was sailing eastward and after a few days it already bypassed Newfoundland, and the crew began to sight large icebergs drifting down from Greenland. When a sailor pointed out a large pod of killer whales, all were amazed by the sight, but the Norwegian passenger/ sailor had a pale blank face of depression, remember these were the same waters he'd sailed through on board the Eriksson.

In Fralhem's eyes were bright white flashes and searches came into his hearing some calling out.

"Vilhelm! Vilhelm!" he heard and recognizing that it was the voice of his old shipmate Korkens from the Eriksson calling out from the sea. Then he felt someone shaking him on the shoulders.

"Mr. Fralhem!" yelled the chief mate, "Take up that line lad!"

Fralhem was back doing his work later that day in the evening when he and most of the crew were bedded down.

Fralhem dreamed he was aboard a small boat that almost

looked like a Viking ship and he was dressed like a warrior. All around him were long, black, dorsal fins.

Fralhem watched when a killer whale had a man in its jaws.

It was Korkens, and then the boat flooded, Fralhem was stuck in his seat and couldn't free himself. Far in the distance came a charging orca. He struggled and struggled for air, and when the killer orca was about to attack the last, he was an open jaw of teeth and a black hole. He screamed and woke up with many sailors staring at him. He apologized and pretended to go back to sleep, but he struggled not do so and just sat up in his bunk all through the night. A week past and Fralhem sleepless night took a toll; it became so bad that the trade ship captain dropped him off at Faroe Island. And now he had to get himself another passage home.

CHAPTER 56

THE CREW'S HOME FRONT

In the summer of 1863, back in America, the civil war was at its height and casualties were mounting by the tens of thousands from both sides. In a telegraph station in Boston was the former sailor Charlie Evekins. Once active and fit, now he was thin, weak and pale. It was unpleasant for him to read the list of battle deaths with hundreds to thousands of young men killed day by day. Soon his well-paid job turned him miserable, dull and him returning home depressed.

Yet at home, he was happy with his beautiful wife.

He and Alasia were trying so hard to have a baby and start a family. Yet Alasia suffered two miscarriages and wanted to wait for more.

Despite the unpopular job, he was glad he was not out in the line of fire and was still in touch with most of his old shipmates.

Connell was now working in a shipyard in Province and would sometimes visit for a drink.

Sween was wounded in the arm by a shrapnel during the siege of Vicksburg and was allowed to return home.

Though severely injured he was lucky enough not to have his arm amputated but was now crippled and would shake uncontrollably for the remainder of his life. Sween did not let it stop him, and he returned to Harvard and eventually became a school teacher in Norwich.

Canonchet returned to whaling; he signed aboard an all Native American vessel from Martha's Vineyard as an officer along with his eldest son Nathan as the cabin boy.

Sam Witty also went back to the sea, but this time in the merchant services going on voyages to Africa around the Ivory Coast. And all he earned he gave it straight to his family for support.

And Prestern. Well, old Prestern was gone, killed on the streets of New York during the draft riots. When the news reached all members of Fralhem's boat crew, they took the news in moment silence and intense sadness at the loss of such a dear good friend.

CHAPTER 57

Going Aft again

Canonchet's whaler returned to port after less than a year in the Spring of 1864 with only 700 barrels of Sperm whale oil, from the Indian Ocean. Despite returning with a fair amount, the crew was paid real small profits, caused by the war and that whale oil was being beaten by the oil coming from the ground in the western states like Pennsylvania and Ohio. Before Canonchet was to serve aboard his ship again as the first mate, the owners sold the vessel, and he lost his opportunity for a better-paid position.

The man did not want to go back to petty jobs as a simple fisherman and wanted his son, Nathan to have his chance at the harpoon.

So, he went to visit Window Branter for help, to find a good insured whaleship that's willing to go out during these hard times. And she did so, with her connections to America's most wealthy shipbuilders.

Her son Cole had got a position on the latest New Bedford whaler, Charlotte Moriana to serve as a midshipman.

The owners were now looking to hire more goodly experienced whalers to take the long three-year voyage and they appointed Mat Canonchet to serve as second mate and his son as his harpooner. On the morning when she was to depart. Mat discovered old shipmates had joined them, Connell signed aboard as master engineer and Witty came back as quartermaster, a position secured for him by the merchant company he transferred from.

Right before the Charlotte was off, the final people came aboard the. Mr. and Mrs. Evekins.

"Great Heavens above! Charlie Evekins!" shouted Connell has taken him in his arms.

"What are you doing Charlie?' asked Cole. "Have you the job station office?"

"Well the station manager laid me off but gave me a good last raise, besides I'm not signing aboard as a whaler," he explained.

"We'll be leaving on a different ship, taking us to Europe," Alasia came over as he spoke. "When we heard old friends signing aboard The Moriana we thought we could say farewell."

"Which part of Europe are you are going to?" asked Witty.

"France," answered Alasia. "Going to look for some relatives of mine."

"Oh good," said Canonchet. "When there, maybe you two could find Fralhem."

"Well we don't know, but we'll see when we get there," she said.

So as the couple exchanged goodbyes with their friends and hugged and kissed as if they were never going to see each other ever again. It was not surprising for Canonchet and the others since they had received the same goodbyes from loved ones and felt good that the two were leaving to go off and find family members, the same thing their savior and leader Fralhem had done. It was just a ploy. Charlie and Alasia were not going to France.

CHAPTER 58

THE CALF'S END

Spending the winter in Torshavn on the Faroe Islands after being ditched by the Canadian trade ship, Fralhem now grew a short burnett beard. Though in his late twenties he felt like an old man when he looked into his shaving mirror.

After his first glimpse of himself in months, he came to recognize someone. So, before he was about to shave, he took out his small leather case that possessed his valued treasure.

This was not money nor gold but a small picture painting of his parents. Looking down at it as they were the faces of beauty, Fralhem now regretted he never looked much at this portrait during his lost time on the whaleboat.

He remembered way back how his mother would nudge him gently with his face to hers and how smooth they were.

Fralhem even regretted that his young brother never had that chance. And he promised to give this picture to him.

Then he turned his eyes to his father. And he saw he was looking more like his old man. He had the same hair and same style, was light bearded and not too thin nor too thick, so he decided not to shave.

That morning the man decided to go off on a hike of the island's valley lands. So, after a small and quiet breakfast of Faroese puffin meat with other whalers and fishermen, Fralhem went off.

Walking out through the cobbled streets near the harbor, he passed by large rows of slain long-finned pilot whales, the best-known prey for the Faroe whaling fishery. New Englanders hunted sperm whales, Faroe Islanders hunted long fins. During the times Fralhem stayed in the inn he shared stories about being aboard the famous Nantucket whaling fleet, but never shared his lost at sea adventure, yet many islanders were amazed with the Norwegian stranger who formally worked aboard American whaleships.

He walked out of town into the countryside with a small branch as a cane. Through the hills, sheep roamed freely.

The snow was light more like a small flurry and less than a foot deep. Fralhem remembered how the winters in the north got really brutal, but since it was not so sorry, he took advantage of this opportunity to stretch his legs.

Coming atop the hills overlooking the harbor he looked down at the docked ships, the town, and Norwegian sea. If he was an artist, he would have stopped to paint the beautiful landscapes.

From over the snow-covered hills, Fralhem made his way to the rocky cliffs of the island's forges. Walking along the edge, he made sitting slags fly off the side.

While walking back down in the afternoon, the Norwegian made it to the shore, and there he saw a swarm of birds in the air. Curious, he began to walk faster down the beach. When it came into his sight he saw a crowd of people mostly armed with flensing tools, so he knew it had to be a whale.

Before he could ask a young man in the group spoke out,

"Hey, it's the man from the American whale ships!"

All turned with smiles to him obviously people had heard his sea tales, and they all told him to come on over and see what they had found washed up. All he could make out of it was they were saying, "A whale! We found a whale!" A bit confused but he moved forward.

Walking through the joyful crowd with pats to the shoulder and back, he paused and saw that it a sperm whale with a familiar marking to the head. It was the very whale that had saved him from drowning, the young sperm whale that he made orphaned and saved both him and his men had now been stabbed to death on the Faroe beach.

All were cheering and laughing as some people danced on the dead whale's body. All the while Fralhem stared into the eye of the poor dead creature.

A quick flashback blew into his mind.

He was back on the island when he and his crew were lost. It was right after he'd taken the rusted lance and informed his crew that he was off to kill the whale that was beached on the rocky shore.

He walked on thinking of that dream he'd had that if he had killed the whale, he wouldn't have survived. And he didn't.

When Fralhem came up to the helpless whale he remembered what he said to it.

"I will not kill you," he said aloud to the whale as it stared at him with its left eye.

He struck the lance into the ground and pushed with all its might trying to get the young whale back in the sea. But he made little to no progress. And he would have got it back in until Evekins and LaCapet came along and helped him.

They pushed the whale with more help from the tide and left the whale swim out free. That memory ran deep in his mind until Fralhem was snapped out of it by a man.

"Hey Norge!" he said, "Here take this."

Fralhem looked that he was handing him and harpoon.

"Go on, take it whaler!" shouted another man. "Take a stab at the beast! Take the honor!"

But Fralhem did not. He just ran off, away from the crowd of savage hunters, who were just laughing at him. It was a long run back to the capital and to his inn room. He cried like a child into his pillow.

CHAPTER 59

FIND ANOTHER EDEN

Around this same time half, a world away, the New Bedford whaler Charlotte Marion made a supply stop off the coast of Ecuador. In a small beach village, the whalers traded for fresh water and food.

When Witty and Connell made their way to the jungle line, taking basket loads of fruit from a farmer they saw a group of locals with two white people.

One was a man, another a woman. As the two shipmates walked pass. The too saw the face of the man.

Both were shocked but kept walking on. It wasn't until they got to the boats the two talked.

"Connell? Did you see what I saw?" Witty asked.

"Yeah, it looked like Charlie," replied the Irishman.

"But it can't be."

Through that whole time, the two just kept wondering yet they tried forgetting about it, especially when it was time to return to the ship. At that time the two refused to believe it was their friend and did not share it with Canonchet.

On top of a jungle mountain, the couple watched as the whaleship sailed off.

"You know my love? I figured when we all parted away,

I believed that somehow, someway our paths will cross again," Alasia said.

"And you were right to love," said her husband with a kiss.

Turns out Charlie and Alasia were never going to France, but to the jungles of South America. They wanted to find a place they could live in peace with no society, just like back on the island.

The couple vanished into the jungle with nothing. They lived like Adam and Eve, free from all trappings of material passions including their clothes even though they knew it would be hard and dangerous. But through what they had gone through when marooned and lost at sea, they feared not and cared not. All they cared about was one another.

When they settled down in a beautiful jungle by the riverside near the border of Peru, they had nothing else to do in their spare time, but love making endlessly through the nights, in a place of peace and beauty.

CHAPTER 60

A SEARCH VOYAGE BEGINS

In June 1864, on the docks of Stavanger Norway, a small dory vessel was docked. The captain of that tiny vessel was once named Fralhem; now he went only by his birth name.

When he came up to the dock's master, he asked for a spot to keep his dinghy. The master asked for his name, to which the stranger answered, "Call me...Membjorg." He said plainly.

And the master put the name on the documents. "Vilhelm Membjorg."

"Well then," said the Dock owner. "Welcome to Norway, Herr Membjorg."

To the end of the docks, were the same streets young Vilhelm had departed from when he left to go to sea. Now he had returned over two decades later.

"I'm here," he said to himself in his head. "My home country. My own people, speaking my native language. I leave the life of the sea behind... of action and adventure for one thing more important my brother. I will find you."

After that, all rang through his head, Vilhelm Membjorg hung his sea hammock over his shoulder, put his pipe in his mouth, his free hand in his pocket and a small leather pouch containing his portraits of his parents, took it out and placed it around his neck.

He walked on laid bricks determined to find his only family, his brother.

Not knowing where Kristopher was or had gone, the only way he could find him was to retrace his past. He would go to the place left his sibling at such an early age and look from there. He'd do it step by step and would not let anything stop him, even if he had to get the king himself to help.

The heroic journey of the former whaleship officer was at an end. But a voyage of family reconnection was now beginning with the first step putting the memories of his shipmates behind him, only to think of one person and one person only Kristopher Membjorg. It was to begin a whole new chapter of his life. There he walked alone through the streets of the city.

End.

CHARACTERS

- Vilhelm "Fralhem" Membjorg: The Norwegian, third mate of the Mako and leader of the boat crew when lost at sea. He needed to find a reason to return and survive.

- Charlemagne "Charlie" Evekins: A common sailor, that helped Fralhem find his purpose to return home. Later became husband to Alasia.

- Alasia LaCapet. French Polynesian who survived years on an island alone till she comes along with Fralhem's crew. Eventually falls in love, then marries Charlie.

- Old Tom Prestern: The Mako's steward and oldest member of Fralhem's boat crew. He is later killed in the Draft Riots of 1863 in New York City.

- Kevin Connell: The Mako's skilled carpenter from Cobh Ireland and member of Fralhem's boat crew.

- Matthew Canonchet: Fralhem's harpooner from the Pequot tribe. The most resourceful member of the crew.

- Owen Sween: The most educated member aboard Fralhem's boat and former university student.

- Samuel Witty: An escaped slave from Louisiana who joins the whaling company to support his family. Closest to Prestern and worked as ship's tailor and sailmaker.

The Mako.

- Jethro Heszits: The German-American cabin boy of the Mako who deserts the voyage, because of Gerard's bad captaincy and desire to go his own way. He reunited with Charlie and Fralhem in Hawaii and returned with them to America later joined the U.S. Navy.

- Isaac Branter: First mate of the Mako that never went looking for Fralhem when he and his boat crew went missing.

- Paul Tisburn: Second mate of the Mako and shipmate to Fralhem who quit whaling and joined the Navy during the Civil War.

- Captain Calais Gerard: the paranoid and unstable captain who tried to save the oil when it caught fire; as a result, he and half his crew were killed in an explosion, sinking the Mako.

- Mr. Timrod: The captain's harpooner, later killed when the Mako blew up.

The RMS Tracy.

- Captain George Buster: The Tracy's commander that saved Fralhem's crew.

- Simon Horatio: A wealthy passenger from Liverpool that brought the story from Fralhem.

- Mr. Forey: An officer of the Tracy.
- Ruth: The stewardess that tended Fralhem.

Others.

- The calf: The young sperm whale whose mother was killed by Fralhem and Tisburn. The calf hauled the whaleboat out to the open sea, returned the boat to the island and saved Fralhem from drowning.
- Captain Altorga: Captain of the Teolacho from Mexico, who helped get Fralhem's crew closer to America.
- Mrs. Pearl Branter: Mr. Branter's wife to widow, who was well connected with politicians.
- Cole Branter: Mr. Branter's son who worked as a telegraph repairman and later joins the whaling fishery.
- Alashanee Canonchet: Matthew's wife from the Narraganset tribe of Rhode Island.
- Nathan Canonchet: Matthew's eldest son who followed in his father's footsteps to become a harpooner.
- Debbie and Denies Connell: Connell's twin sisters.
- Father Chapple: Tended the funeral of the first mate, Mr. Branter, and the wedding of Charlie and Alasia.
- Lars Korkens: Fralhem's shipmate aboard the Erickson. Who was killed by an orca.

- Kristopher Membjorg: Vilhelm's youngest brother. The only person in the world that gave Vilhelm a reason to survive and return to Norway.

- Captain Leif: Captain of the Erickson who died of illness just before they reached land after being rescued.

- Andrea Prestern: Tom Prestern's daughter and mother to Dawn.

NORWEGIAN WORD TRANSLATIONS

- Mine venns: my friends.
- A nein: oh no.
- Ga lop: Go run!
- Hold kjeft: shut up!
- Herregud: Good God.
- Ja: yes, or yeah.
- Ynkelig: pitiful.
- Tosk: Fool.
- Farvel: farewell.

ABOUT THE AUTHOR

I was born in Poughkeepsie New York in 1996. I was raised mostly by my mother and grew up eight years in Saugerties, New York. We later moved to Hopewell Jct New York and stayed there ever since. I was diagnosed with Asperger syndrome which is high functioning autism when I was an infant. I also have Dyslexia making reading and writing a challenge my whole life. I didn't even start reading and writing well until I was eleven years old.

In my school years, I attended special education classes until I decided to drop out of High school in 2013 when I was seventeen-year-old and earned a TASC (Test Assessing Secondary Completion) diploma a year later. I now work to support my mother and grandmother. Writing became a real good hobby for me; ever since I learned to read I became real interested in history and literary work. I first began writing stories in 2012 when I was in special ed classes in High School and finished my very first book in 2017. Writing helps me express my mind, thoughts and imagination, helps me relieve stress and I can express myself in the stories that I write like a painter or a musician, I use writing as an outlet.

Printed in the United States
By Bookmasters